FIGHT TO THE FINISH

A bell rang and Slocum stumbled into the middle of the ring. He circled, trying to keep the sun out of his eyes, but Quinn was cagey and knew all the tricks. Dirt under his shuffling feet kicked up small clouds of choking dust.

"I'm gonna kill you, Slocum."

Slocum didn't rise to the challenge. He knew the tricks. If he hesitated, if his attention drifted for just a second when Quinn taunted him, the other man would strike. Slocum blocked two punches to his face. A roar went up from the crowd.

The fight was on.

DON'T MISS THESE
ALL-ACTION WESTERN SERIES
FROM THE BERKLEY PUBLISHING GROUP

***THE GUNSMITH** by J. R. Roberts*
Clint Adams was a legend among lawmen, outlaws, and ladies. They called him . . . the Gunsmith.

***LONGARM** by Tabor Evans*
The popular long-running series about U.S. Deputy Marshal Long—his life, his loves, his fight for justice.

***SLOCUM** by Jake Logan*
Today's longest-running action Western. John Slocum rides a deadly trail of hot blood and cold steel.

***BUSHWHACKERS** by B. J. Lanagan*
An action-packed series by the creators of Longarm! The rousing adventures of the most brutal gang of cutthroats ever assembled—Quantrill's Raiders.

JAKE LOGAN

SLOCUM AT SCORPION BEND

JOVE BOOKS, NEW YORK

If you purchased this book without a cover, you should be aware that this book is stolen property. It was reported as "unsold and destroyed" to the publisher, and neither the author nor the publisher has received any payment for this "stripped book."

SLOCUM AT SCORPION BEND

A Jove Book / published by arrangement with
the author

PRINTING HISTORY
Jove edition / May 1999

All rights reserved.
Copyright © 1999 by Penguin Putnam Inc.
This book may not be reproduced in whole or part,
by mimeograph or other means, without permission.
For information address: The Berkley Publishing Group,
a division of Penguin Putnam Inc.,
375 Hudson Street, New York, New York 10014.

The Penguin Putnam Inc. World Wide Web site address is
http://www.penguinputnam.com

ISBN: 0-515-12510-5

A JOVE BOOK®
Jove Books are published by The Berkley Publishing Group,
a division of Penguin Putnam Inc.,
375 Hudson Street, New York, New York 10014.
JOVE and the "J" design
are trademarks belonging to Penguin Putnam Inc.

PRINTED IN THE UNITED STATES OF AMERICA

10 9 8 7 6 5 4 3 2 1

JAKE LOGAN

SLOCUM AT SCORPION BEND

1

The thunder of hooves behind him on the trail to Scorpion Bend, Wyoming, caused John Slocum to reach instinctively for the ebony-handled Colt Navy slung in his cross-draw holster. He looked around the narrow draw and saw no escape. Visions of a posse hot on his trail flashed across his mind. Then he pushed them away. He had left *that* trouble far behind him in Colorado, along with a dead gambler and a distraught woman hungering for his scalp. Whatever the reason for the pursuit along the narrow, winding trail through the sheer-walled pass in the mountains, it had nothing to do with the law.

He hoped.

Slocum had too many Wanted posters floating around the West with his picture on them to rest easy—or to be complacent.

"Come on," he said, patting his sorrel's neck. "It'll be a climb for you, but it'll be worth it." He dismounted and tugged at the reins of the increasingly skittish horse. The pounding hooves behind him became louder, more insistent. Slocum jerked at the reins in his hand, and got his horse moving up a gravel-strewn trail off the main road—if the double-rutted path could be called a road.

Twenty feet up into the rocks was as far as Slocum

got before the dozen mounted men, hunkered down next to their horses' necks, came riding like the wind. They bumped each other, trying to force each other into the rocks and off the road, but aside from this nothing disturbed their mindless rush.

Slocum relaxed a mite after the clot of riders passed by. The dust choked him, and he had to wipe it off his face and out of his watering eyes. But relief flooded him. Those weren't lawmen. He wasn't certain what they were, other than damned fools trying to kill their horses in the stifling canyon heat, but they weren't after *him*.

"Sort of makes me want to ride somewhere other than Scorpion Bend," Slocum told his horse. "If the whole town is chock full of dolts like them, we're better off sleeping under the stars another night." Even as the words slipped from his lips, Slocum knew he would press on to Scorpion Bend for a meal he hadn't fixed, a hot bath, and a soft bed, even if he had to wrestle the bedbugs and deal with those riders.

Any band of men who rode like that had to work up a powerful thirst. They'd drink until they staggered, get drunk and mean, and start shooting up the saloon. He had seen it too many times.

But seldom had he seen men so intent on riding without a purpose.

This caused him to sit on a rock and wait a spell to see if anyone—or anything—pursued the riders. Ten minutes after the echoing from the horses' hooves had died down, Slocum had still heard nothing but the faint whine of wind through the rocks around him. The day was turning hot, even for a Wyoming summer. He looked up at the burning sun, wiped more grime and sweat from his face, then fastened his now-damp blue bandanna around his neck again.

"Time to get on into town," Slocum told his sorrel. The horse snorted and tried to rear. He held it in check. Truth to tell, he was more than a little curious about the riders and the big hurry they'd shown along this trail to nowhere special. Not one of the men had noticed him standing in the rocks, or even the spoor he had left along the canyon road. The hot wind he had experienced on the flats leading to the mountain pass might have erased some of his tracks in the dry dust, but after he had started along the chute through the mountains, even this had died down.

He mounted and rode at a more leisurely pace than that of the men who had passed him by in a twinkling. The hot wind blowing harder into his face after another half hour of riding told him he was getting near the end of this rocky chasm. A few minutes later, the odor from Scorpion Bend hit him full in the face.

Civilization, or what passed for it in the center of the wilds of Wyoming.

Scorpion Bend sat like a wooden jewel in the middle of a large green bowl. Good pastureland surrounded the town, and a small stream meandered down from higher in the mountains to furnish abundant drinking water. From the number of saloons he could see, Slocum reckoned the town had a population of four or five hundred. What kept it going was something else. He didn't see any evidence of mining. That left ranching. If he found himself so inclined, he might look for a job on a spread and stay around for a few more months. Scorpion Bend didn't look like too bad a place to dally.

For a while.

A big canvas banner stretched from one side of the main street to the other. All it said in sloppily painted red letters was BIG RACE. For the middle of the day Scorpion Bend seemed especially lively. Men came and went from the saloons, and womenfolk moved from one store to another. Something had brought them to town for a big celebration.

Slocum figured it had to be the "big race."

He swung his long leg over the saddle and dropped to

the dusty street. Walking slowly to get the kinks out of his legs and some circulation back into his butt, he tethered his horse and saw it could reach the watering barrel outside a tent saloon. He wiped more dust from his face, then ducked low, went into the dim canvas-walled gin mill, and waited for his eyes to adapt to the lower light level inside.

The smell of stale beer hit him like a hammer and made his mouth water. It had been too long since he had downed a frothy brew or a shot of whiskey or even that Mexican rotgut they called tequila. This was one of the penalties of being on the run—no time to stop and appreciate the simpler pleasures.

"Beer and lunch for a dime," called out the barkeep.

"Done," Slocum said, reaching into his shirt pocket and finding a silver dollar. He dropped it on the broad plank supported by two sawhorses that formed the bar. Before the coin had stopped its dulcet ringing, the bartender had scooped it up and replaced it with a mug of beer and a sandwich on a plate.

"I want change from that," Slocum said pointedly.

"Double or nothing?" suggested the barkeep, a hopeful note in his words.

Slocum hesitated. He didn't have much more than that cartwheel to his name, but something about the barkeep and the atmosphere in Scorpion Bend made him nod.

"High-low or just a flip of the coin?" asked the barkeep.

"No need to break out a fresh deck of marked cards," Slocum said. He motioned for the barkeep to come closer. "You flip and I'll call."

The silver dollar caught every ray of light inside the saloon as it spun over and over.

"Tails," Slocum said, his hand moving fast to clamp the barkeep's down to the plank. He lifted the man's hand away from the coin and smiled. "I win," he said.

"Here's your dime," the barkeep said. "And the beer and food's on the house."

"The bet was for the silver dollar," Slocum said.

"No, no, it wasn't. It was just for your beer."

"Consider the other ninety cents your tip," Slocum said, not wanting to argue. His belly grumbled from hunger and the beer was cold enough to whet his thirst for more.

"You got a way about you, mister," said a woman's gravelly voice. Slocum turned to look at the woman, maybe pushing fifty from her gray hair and lined face, but with eyes that sparkled and a manner that bespoke of still enjoying life to the fullest.

"What? That I let him sucker me out of the rest of the bet? If I'd lost, he would have kept the dollar."

"Jed's like that," she said, pushing a strand of hair from her eyes. "I'm Miss Maggie, and I own this place, such as it is."

"Pleased to meet you," Slocum said, touching the brim of his Stetson politely.

"You're a gambling man. I can tell. You want to lay a bet?" she asked.

"On the big race?" Slocum asked, guessing.

"What else? The Annual Scorpion Bend Horse Race and Pissing Contest is about the biggest thing to bet on in the entire territory."

"After this beer, I'd be more inclined to enter the latter," Slocum said, draining the mug and pushing it across the bar for a refill.

"No bet? I'm backing Mormon Will this year. He can't lose. The man rides like he was born in the saddle. I think he's part Arapaho from the way he controls his horse. Put in a bet now and you might walk away with a couple thousand."

"What are the odds?"

"No odds right now. The first leg of the race is this weekend. Anyone with a ticket on any of the first ten finishers can sell the ticket for a princely sum. Then in mid-week the field's reduced to five, and on the following Saturday the last race determines the winner."

"So everyone buys a ticket, the money's thrown into a pot, and everyone holding a ticket on the winner divvies up the pot?"

"That's it. Might be five thousand dollars a ticket," Miss Maggie said.

Slocum let out a low whistle. "That's mighty big money."

"The real money's made on the side bets. Since Mormon Will's the favorite, he might not get more than three- or four-to-one odds."

"Mighty high for the favorite," Slocum pointed out.

"This isn't just *any* race, mister. This is the Scorpion Bend race."

"You're saying it might get dangerous because of so much money changing hands?" He saw how a man's ticket might go up in value should an opposing rider not finish the race. "How much goes into the big boodle?"

"Might be as much as fifty thousand dollars. We charge a hundred a head for a rider to enter, and we got almost eighty right now. Ten dollars a ticket on any rider of your choice, buy as many as you want."

"No need to buy more 'n one, from what you say," Slocum said, smiling crookedly. "I got no reason to disbelieve you when you say Mormon Will is going to win."

Miss Maggie laughed. The sound was joyous but like rocks grinding together. "You have a wit as well as a quick hand," she said. Her eyes dropped to the worn handle of his six-shooter and the easy way he carried it. "I saw how you moved when you slapped Jed's hand down on the bar."

"I'm not a hired gunman," Slocum said tersely. "I'm just a cowboy passing through."

"Passing through to where? This is the end of the

earth, 'cept for the big race," she said. Miss Maggie motioned to Jed for a bottle and two shot glasses. "My personal bottle." She expertly poured two drinks, not spilling a drop. Slocum could almost believe this *was* her own bottle from the way she handled it.

"To what do I owe this honor?" he asked, taking the shot glass. The smell of the whiskey took him back to days on the Mississippi and real Kentucky bourbon.

"This is Billy Taylor's Reserve, 'bout the finest I can get out here. Drink up." The woman tossed back the drink expertly, then licked her lips as if she could spend the rest of the day working on the bottle. Her eyes darted from the bottle back to Slocum.

He drank the smooth whiskey and expressed his regard for the quality.

"A real Southern gentleman you are too. I'm a good judge of men, since I've been married five times," she said. "You're honest. I can tell."

"Don't go making claims you can't back up," Slocum said. This caused Miss Maggie to laugh again.

"You see real clear concerning the race. A little mishap and a rider's chance for glory is gone for another year. I want Mormon Will to have a fair shot at winning—I know he can if the race isn't rigged. I can see to that part, but what I can't see to is some yahoo busting him up before the race. Or worse."

"Men have been killed before the race?"

"And after winning the first leg," Miss Maggie said soberly. "I'll pay you ten dollars a day, room and board, no whiskey, to watch after Will."

"Bodyguard?"

Miss Maggie nodded.

Slocum considered a half dozen things, all at once. He had nowhere in particular to go. Mostly, he just didn't want to be down in Colorado with its passel of lawmen all wanting to stick his head in a noose. From what he had seen of Scorpion Bend, the town was wide open and the law wasn't too concerned with Wanted posters. Everyone concentrated completely on the big race. He had to smile at the sign flapping outside in the hot afternoon breeze since it summed up everything he had seen about Scorpion Bend.

"That's better pay than I'd get punching cattle," he said.

"Harder, more dangerous," Miss Maggie said.

"You've never tried to stop a stampede," Slocum said.

Miss Maggie laughed. "And you've never seen how vicious men get when it gets time for the race. I'm not looking to run you off, but this isn't going to be a picnic."

"Mormon Will?" Slocum said, rolling the name over and over and then letting it slip off his tongue, as if sampling more of Miss Maggie's fine whiskey.

"That's what he calls himself. Might be a summer name, but no one's asking, no one much cares."

"Least of all you. He's a good rider?"

"The best. You can start right away. Mormon Will's ready to go for a practice run down the canyon and back."

"My horse might not be able to keep up."

"Then tell him to practice outside of town, down in Meegan's Meadow."

"Done," Slocum said, thrusting out his hand. Miss Maggie shook it with a grip firmer than most men.

"Get your carcass on out of here and watch over him. You can't miss him. He's a big galoot, half a head taller 'n you, and big. Really big."

Slocum ran his finger around the rim of the shot glass and sampled the last of the whiskey, then left the canvas tent saloon to find Mormon Will. It didn't take long, because the giant of a man was arguing with the stable owner.

"What's the trouble?" asked Slocum, coming up. The

owner of the livery was a midget compared to Mormon Will, but he wasn't backing down. He shoved out his chest and banged it against Mormon Will's immense belly.

"He's refusin' to pay up," the livery man told Slocum. "Owes a week's keep for his nag."

"You go talk to Miss Maggie 'bout it," said Mormon Will. The giant smelled of alcohol, making Slocum wonder where the man's handle came from. Slocum had never known a practicing Mormon to drink at all, much less as much as this one obviously had in the past few hours.

"I ain't goin' nowhere. You'd take the horse and never be seen again." The livery man backed off, rubbed the stubble on his chin, and said, "Maybe that's not such a bad idea. I kin charge twice what yer payin' when the rest of them fools get into town to race."

"How much?" asked Slocum.

"A dollar."

Slocum handed over his silver dollar, thinking he would add this to his bill with Miss Maggie. Right now he wanted nothing more than to get the practice session over so he could grab some sleep. He had been in the saddle a long time and needed to rest. More than that, the heat was getting oppressive in Scorpion Bend. A cool meadow would be far more relaxing than any town.

"Much obliged, stranger." Mormon Will thrust out his hand. Slocum knew what to expect and clamped down hard, matching Mormon Will's grasp ounce for ounce.

"Miss Maggie hired me to watch your back. You race, I make sure no one shoots you."

"I'm way behind on my trainin' schedule," Mormon Will said. He saddled and rode out. Slocum fetched his own horse and trotted to catch up. Mormon Will's horse was a big, midnight black stallion suitable for a man of his height and girth. With a smaller rider, that horse might run all day and far into the night.

Outside town, Slocum asked, "Where are you training today? Miss Maggie said you might try some meadow."

"The road. I always ride on the road to get this nag used to the shadows and holes along the race route." Mormon Will pointed back down the narrow canyon Slocum had just traversed getting to Scorpion Bend.

Slocum nodded slowly. That explained the men on horses and their breakneck riding. They were practicing for the race too.

"Can't keep up with your horse," Slocum said. "Don't know how well I can watch after you if you're out of sight."

"Jist follow my dust," Mormon Will said with a laugh. He put his heels into the black stallion's sides. The horse reared, pawed at the air, then dropped its front legs and took off like a shot. Slocum started after Mormon Will, not even trying to keep up. The man could outdistance him and his sorrel with little effort.

Content to trot along, Slocum entered the narrow chasm and began to taste the dust from the hard-galloping horse ahead. He kept moving, feeling like the tortoise in the story about the tortoise and the hare. He didn't push his horse—until the gunshots rang out.

"Come on," Slocum said, using his spurs on his sorrel. The horse raced forward, forcing Slocum to bend low and let the animal have its head. He reined back when he came to Mormon Will standing beside his downed stallion.

"They shot Ole Rocket," he said. "Those sons of bitches shot my horse!"

Slocum grabbed for his rifle and pulled it from the saddle scabbard. He levered a round into the Winchester and scanned the tumble of rocks all around for the gunman.

"Where'd the shot come from?" he asked, seeing nothing. For some reason, Slocum looked to see if Mormon Will carried a side arm. He didn't. There hadn't been a rifle slung at the side of his saddle either. The man was unarmed and not likely to have killed his own horse, for whatever reason. Tears ran down the man's cheeks.

"Up there. Ahead," Mormon Will said. He knelt beside his horse and cradled the animal's head. This convinced Slocum that the man had had nothing to do with killing his own horse.

"We'd better get out of here," Slocum said. His sharp green eyes scanned the rocks, but came up with nothing. There had been only a single shot to bring down the horse. That meant either a lucky shot, or a sniper who knew his business. Slocum had been a sharpshooter during the war, and had been one of the best. He knew how hard a shot like the one made on Mormon Will's horse was.

"How?" Mormon Will said. "You want me to walk?"

"Get your saddle. We can sling that behind me, but my sorrel's not going to support us both."

Mormon Will worked to get his tack off the dead horse, already drawing flies in the hot Wyoming afternoon sun. Slocum wiped futilely at the sweat pouring down his own face and causing his shirt to glue itself to his body. A sense of impending doom welled up. A single shot? Might have been an accident, he told himself. But he didn't think so.

"Hurry up," Slocum said. He grunted as he wrestled Mormon Will's saddle into place behind his saddle. The man was so tall his head topped that of the sorrel.

"Miss Maggie ain't gonna like this, not at all."

"I'll buy you a drink when we tell her," Slocum said. "She said you were the best rider. She can find you another horse."

"But Ole Rocket was the best," moaned Mormon Will.

Slocum saw the glint of sunlight off a rifle barrel an

12   JAKE LOGAN

instant before he heard the sharp crack. The report echoed down the canyon until it vanished. He rose in his stirrups, and got off three fast shots intended to drive the sniper down rather than kill him.

"Take cover," Slocum cried, struggling to keep his horse under control. When he didn't get an answer, he glanced over his shoulder. He went cold inside when he saw the giant of a man stretched out, a bullet hole in the side of his head. Mormon Will had been killed instantly with a single shot.

"Now how am I going to tell Miss Maggie she's lost both her best horse and her best rider?" he wondered aloud. Slocum dismounted and went to cover, worrying more for his own hide than about what to tell the saloon owner. The sniper in the rocks ahead was one damned fine marksman.

2

Slocum sweated in the hot sun, hunting for another hint to where the sniper lay in the rocks up the canyon. He considered mounting and galloping the hell out of there, but that would expose his back to a man who was about the best marksman Slocum had come across in years. Two shots, two deaths.

"Or did he miss with the first shot and hit the horse by accident?" Slocum wondered aloud. It made no sense to kill the horse if Mormon Will was considered the rider to beat. Kill the rider, destroy Miss Maggie's chance of having a spot in the top ten come Wednesday. That made a good deal of sense to Slocum.

Whatever the target, the sniper had done some good shooting at the range. Slocum mopped sweat, pulled down the brim of his hat, and watched carefully. Then he pressed his ear to the ground to detect any vibration of a departing horse. He saw nothing; he heard nothing. That made him even edgier.

After twenty minutes, he knew he had to make a move. He was getting to the point of having more cotton than tongue in his mouth. If he didn't get more than a swallow of water soon and find some shade, he was going to start shooting at hallucinations. Still, the reason he had been such a good sniper for the Confederacy was patience. Others would jump around like jackrabbits on a hot griddle, giving away their positions, getting flushed from good spots through nothing but nervousness. He knew all the justifications to stay put.

Slocum moved.

Expecting a bullet to rip through him at any instant, he mounted and rode slowly in the direction of the sniper. Nothing. He got closer. The hackles on his neck rose, and he shivered in spite of the taxing heat. Every second he remained in the Wyoming sun, he lost a little more strength.

Then he was past the point in the rocks where the killer had lain. Slocum considered checking the spot, hunting for spoor, maybe finding a trail. Then he held out his hand and saw how shaky he had become. He had been dog-tired when he'd ridden out with Mormon Will. Now he was thirsty to the point of passing out, as well as exhausted physically and emotionally.

He rode back into Scorpion Bend, wondering how Miss Maggie was going to take the news that her newly hired bodyguard had failed—terribly.

"Land 'o mercy, Slocum, you're a fright," Miss Maggie said as he wobbled into the saloon. He dropped into a chair. She called to Jed to fetch a bottle.

"Water," Slocum said, his voice hardly more than a hoarse whisper. "I can't handle tarantula juice yet." He took the dirty glass filled with muddy water and downed it. It tasted sweeter than any spring runoff water coming from high in the Rockies.

"You look a fright, but I think there's something more, isn't there?" said Miss Maggie.

Slocum related the story, finishing, "I left him out there. He deserves a burial. And if you can rustle up a posse, we might track down the varmint responsible."

"Varmint?" snorted Miss Maggie. Her lips thinned to a razor slash. "There's not a one of these whoresons who wouldn't kill Mormon Will. A dozen of 'em might have had it in for Will. That's why you were hired."

"I'm sorry," Slocum said.

"There wasn't much you could do, from the sound of it." Miss Maggie frowned. Slocum worried she wouldn't believe him, that the saloon owner might think he had killed Mormon Will for his own ends. With so much money floating around Scorpion Bend, any combination of money and treachery was possible.

Slocum downed another glass of water and began thinking about whiskey. The way his mouth still felt like the inside of a cotton bale, he knew he had to get some more water. And his horse needed its fill too. And food. For both of them.

"I promised," Slocum said. "I said I wouldn't let anyone hurt Mormon Will, and now he's dead."

"So Southern gent that you are, you're feeling mighty poorly about this?" she asked. A smile crossed her lips, replacing the one of grim determination that had been there before. Slocum wasn't sure he wanted to hear what she was going to suggest, but there was nothing he could do to stop her from suggesting it.

Or him from accepting.

"I furnish a horse and you ride. You said you were a cowpuncher. That means you've done some bronco busting in your day."

"There's a difference between breaking a horse and playing jockey. I've raced with some Navajos at a chicken pull, but—"

"They beat you?" Miss Maggie laughed. "You never gave up trying, though, even if your horse was dying under you? No, you didn't," she said, answering her own question. "I know your type, Slocum, and you're what I need—what I *want*—for a rider."

"All I can promise is to do my best."

"I have a hunch it might be better than Mormon Will could have done."

"That was one fine horse he rode."

"I'll see you get another one—and Black Velvet isn't going to end up swayback. You're nowhere near the weight to carry that Mormon Will was. Rocket was the stronger of the pair, so Mormon Will got him. But Black Velvet and you are a match made in heaven." Miss Maggie laughed at this. Slocum felt tired and not a little wary of agreeing to ride in the Scorpion Bend race. But what choice did he have?

Slocum yawned, stretched, and stepped out into the street, having slept all afternoon in the tiny second-floor hotel room. If it hadn't been for Miss Maggie, he would have been sleeping in the stables. She was well respected and people around town did what she asked. He felt worlds better, as if he could lick his weight in wildcats as soon as he got a bite to eat. Scorpion Bend had not settled down during the heat of the day, and now that the sun was setting behind the distant peak—Arapaho Peak he had heard it called—it was downright pleasant and everyone came out to do their business.

And talk about the race.

Slocum had started for the small cafe down the street, one that didn't look as if it would poison most of its customers, when he heard a heated argument from the doorway of the Ranchers Bank. A lovely young woman in a worn but clean gingham dress clutched a banker's arm and pleaded with him.

"I tell you, Miss Decker, there is nothing I can do."

"You can give me time to get the money. My pa's laid up and can't work. Give me more time. I can get the money, I swear."

"How?" asked the banker, jerking his arm free of her grip. "Bring in a crop in the next few days? Put that no-account brother of yours to work? Wait for Almighty God on High to come down and give you a pile of money? All of those are about equally likely to happen."

SLOCUM AT SCORPION BEND 17

"Until after the race," she pleaded. Slocum saw she was a handsome brunette, her wide-spaced brown eyes imploring, and she was having no luck at all with the banker.

"So you can bet away what little money you have left?"

"Why not? Why not let me see what can be done?"

"I—" The banker shook his head, took a deep breath, then said, "I'm a fool, Miss Decker. There's no reason for me to do this, but you can have ten days to raise the money. Not one second longer!"

"Thank you," she said, pumping his hand. "I knew you had a heart, no matter what everyone else says."

This seemed to please the banker. He smiled crookedly and said, "Don't go tellin' anyone else. They'll want an extension on their loans too." With that, he put on his tall silk hat, straightened the lapels of his expensive gray suit, and walked off into the gathering twilight, using his walking stick to whack at dogs in the street.

The lovely brunette saw Slocum's interest. She smiled slightly, nodded in his direction, and started off. Slocum matched her stride and walked alongside.

"I hope you don't think me too forward, but I overheard your conversation with the banker. You seem quite determined."

"I am." She looked at him from the corner of her eyes. "You know anything about farming?"

"Done a bit in my day," Slocum said, "but the banker's right. You won't bring in a crop right now. Takes a lot of hard work."

"Nothing Frank's likely to put up with," she said.

"Frank?"

"My brother. Excuse me, sir. I am Rachel Decker." She smiled prettily. Slocum introduced himself, touching the brim of his dusty Stetson. "My brother is a ne'er-do-well, and my father is laid up. I am in serious need of someone to help out on the farm. If you are not caught up in all this farce about the big race, I—'' She bit off her query when she saw his expression. "Oh, you *are* involved in the race."

"Seems like it," Slocum said, considering her offer. "How would you pay me if you can't even make the mortgage payment?"

"I . . . I am facing the truth of the matter, Mr. Slocum. If I fix up the buildings, I can sell it for that much more. Payment would be out of the proceeds for the farm, the house, and everything that goes with it."

"That might not leave you very much."

Rachel shrugged. "So be it then. All I hope to do is get something for the farm before my brother gambles it all away."

From the saloons came the roar of boisterous drunks and games of chance running their course.

"Bucking the tiger is no way to live, unless you know the odds," Slocum said. He had done his share of gambling at faro, on both sides of the deck.

"My brother often cannot remember his way home. He also drinks," she said primly.

Slocum considered doing some honest work, then thought of the obligation he owed Miss Maggie. He had been hired to safeguard her investment in Mormon Will, and he had failed within an hour of taking the job. He wasn't much of a rider when it came to racing, but she held a claim on his time. And the money dangled in front of him was nothing less than astounding.

He might win five thousand dollars or more if he bested the others in the race. From what Slocum figured, Miss Maggie stood to make a pile of money if he simply finished among the top ten riders. A ticket on him would go up almost ten times in value if that happened. From what he had seen of the others practicing their racing skills, he could beat them walking away. They were too aggressive, didn't know how to pace their horses, and had way too much weight and way too little skill riding in their saddles.

Slocum had to admit he had done some fancy racing in his day—mostly to outrun posses.

But some in the race were willing to kill to win. He had seen that firsthand as he'd watched Mormon Will die in the Wyoming sun. Slocum had to be honest. Even with a strong horse, his chance of winning wasn't too good. Working for Rachel Decker gave him a decent, if low-paying, job.

More than that, she was about the prettiest woman he had seen in some time.

"Why doesn't your beau help out?" Slocum asked.

Rachel Decker's smile vanished, replaced by a coldness that chilled Slocum's soul. "The Decker family is something of a pariah in these parts. No one will have anything to do with us. My pa hasn't been the most upstanding citizen, and Frank is certainly following in his footsteps."

"The sins of the father carry to his daughter?" Slocum asked gently.

"Ask around, Mr. Slocum. You'll find the answer to that is yes. Good day, sir." Rachel stalked off. Slocum let her go. She had spirit and seemed to be swimming against the current in Scorpion Bend. It might be better for her to make a break from her family and start over elsewhere.

He considered her offer as he made his way to Miss Maggie's saloon. An extra section in the tent had been opened up to take care of the overflow crowd pressing in. Slocum edged around the flapping tent wall until he saw the owner and caught Miss Maggie's eye. She came over, a glass in her hand.

"You ready to sign on, Slocum?" she asked without so much as a "Howdy, how are you?"

"Never done anything like this before," he said truthfully.

"The ten-dollars-a-day offer is gone," she said. "I'll give you a thousand dollars if you make it into the final five."

"What if I get to the final ten?" he asked.

"Twenty-five dollars a day, use of the horse, room and board, and nothing more. You have to deliver for me to get the big money."

Slocum knew she would win a wad of greenbacks just on betting on a dark horse in the race. If he made the cut at the final ten, a ticket on him might go up more than ten times in value. A thousand dollars might be chicken feed.

"Course, you can always bet on yourself," she said. Then the woman fixed him with her steely gaze. "And if I find you're betting on anyone else and then losing to him, I'll cut your heart out personally."

"I wouldn't throw the race," Slocum said. "I might not take your offer, but I'm not the kind to cheat you."

"I believe you, Slocum. You *are* a Southern gentleman, under that rough exterior. But you make it sound like you have a better offer. Who made it? I'll dicker."

"Wasn't better, not in terms of money," Slocum said. "Just appeals more to me."

"You can have a whale of a lot of appeal with a thick wad of greenbacks riding high in your pocket," she pointed out. Miss Maggie finished the whiskey in her glass, then set it down on a table as if staking out her territory. "Let me know soon. I can get another rider, but it might take some doing."

"All right," Slocum said. The saloon owner went to a table of gamblers, then joined in a hand of five-card stud. Slocum studied the older woman a spell, then turned to the bar and worked at sipping on a cool beer while he thought.

Money and lots of it would be his if he reached the finals of the horse race. On the other hand, he wouldn't get but a few dollars for his trouble if he didn't finish in the top ten in the first day's race. From the look of some of the men in the saloon, they were experienced riders and knew all the tricks.

Rachel Decker's piddling offer of a few dollars for a lot of hard work sounded more attractive by the minute as Slocum thought on it. She had her troubles, worked on them, and seemed honest and straightforward. Slocum had been down on his luck and was willing to help out. It didn't hurt any that Rachel was one mighty fine-looking woman.

As he brought the beer mug to his lips, someone jostled his elbow. He spilled some of the amber liquid down his shirt. Irritated, Slocum turned, expecting to confront a drunk. The man beside him had obviously bumped into him on purpose, and now stood with his feet square, shoulders loose, and hand resting lightly on the holster at his side.

"You're mighty clumsy," the man said.

"You owe me an apology," Slocum said. "You bumped into me."

"That's a lie."

A hush settled on the saloon and men started leaving, going under the tent flaps and out the front doors. Trouble was brewing and if lead started flying, they didn't want to be anywhere near it.

The man facing him down was a gunman and used to killing. Slocum read that in the hot eyes and the stance. He couldn't see the six-shooter at the man's side, but he suspected it was well-used, worn, and able to deliver a .44 slug to his gut if he so much as moved a muscle.

Slocum wasn't sure he could take the man. Maybe. Probably. But he wasn't sure.

"What's your quarrel with me?" Slocum asked.

"You just called me a liar. I don't take that from any man. You going to draw or you going to crawl like a lily-livered snake?"

"Mighty crowded in here," Slocum said. "Might be

22   JAKE LOGAN

you just bumped me and couldn't help yourself. No disgrace in that." He wanted to see how far the gunman would go to pick a fight.

"You said I did it on purpose. You backing down? Were you lyin' before? That figures. A lying, low-down snake." The man's fingers began curling and uncurling at his side now. He was winding himself up like a cheap watch, ready to explode at the first sign that Slocum was going for his six-gun.

"I'll buy you a drink, and we can talk this over," Slocum volunteered, knowing the answer before it left the man's lips.

"I don't drink with an owlhoot who called me a liar. You going to draw or you going to let everyone in here know you're a coward?" Both the gunman's hands were twitching now. He was getting tense, a raw nerve that would explode at the slightest provocation.

Slocum bided his time and said nothing. He didn't look away from the hot gaze, but he didn't back down either.

"Well?" the man said. "I'm going to shoot you where you stand, whether you draw or not, if you don't apologize."

"All right," said Slocum, still playing for time.

"You're apologizing?" The gunman was startled at this, and it broke his fierce concentration on killing.

"Take it however you want." Slocum still didn't look away. He was keyed up too, but didn't show it. If the gunfighter made a move, Slocum would have his Colt Navy out and firing, but the man stepped back and looked around.

"You all heard him. The son of a bitch is running off." The gunman laughed harshly, turned, and started to leave. He paused at the door for a moment, glared at Slocum, then vanished into the night.

The noise rose all around. Miss Maggie came to Slocum's side.

"You know who that was?"

"Nope."

"Cletus Quinn's his name. He's about the orneriest backshooting son of a buck in these parts. Claims he has killed six men."

"Six?" Slocum wondered how many *he* had killed. He couldn't even remember—and that worried him more than the men he had put six feet under.

"He's racing," she said. "You did well to chase him off that way. All he wanted was to frighten you."

"Do tell," said Slocum acidly. He took the whiskey Jed pushed across the bar and downed it in a single gulp. The fiery liquor burned all the way down his gullet and pooled in his belly.

"Did it work?" she asked. "You going to race for me or take that other job?"

"*He* wanted me out of the race?" Slocum asked. "How many others has he tried to scare off?"

"More 'n one, I reckon," said Miss Maggie, "but you're the first he faced down. That means he thinks you're real competition in the race."

"I'll ride for you," Slocum said. No man ran him off, especially the likes of Quinn. Besides, he stood to make a lot of money if he bet carefully and had even a smidgeon of luck come his way.

3

"This is quite a horse," Slocum said, moving cautiously around the animal to keep it from rearing and kicking the daylights out of him. It might have been the twin to the black stallion Mormon Will had ridden to his death on.

"Don't want you letting anyone see you on Black Velvet until tomorrow morning," Miss Maggie warned. "That's not a problem, is it? I want to spring you on the other racers."

Slocum had avoided another run-in with Cletus Quinn by a hair the night before. He wasn't afraid of the man as long as he faced him, but Slocum had heard rumors about how some of the six Quinn claimed as his victims might have had a bullet or two pumped into their backs first. Slocum wasn't sure if Quinn was the unknown rifleman out on the trail who had plugged Mormon Will, but he wouldn't put it past the man. Quinn wanted to win the race as much for the prestige as for the heap of money going with it.

"I can handle him," Slocum said. He blinked, wondering if he'd answered Miss Maggie's question or an unasked one about Cletus Quinn. Slocum smiled slightly.

The answer was the same to both questions. He could handle anything that came his way.

"Black Velvet's a spirited mount," Miss Maggie said. "He was too small for Mormon Will. And there was something else. Mormon Will chose Rocket because he was the less frisky of the two."

"How much do I get for finishing in the top ten?" Slocum asked.

He saw the woman turn cagey. "Twenty-five a day and then the thousand dollars I promised when you get into the final five. Of course, there's nothing to keep you from buying a few tickets on yourself. That might make it worth your while getting into the top ten."

Slocum nodded. He already had five tickets in his pocket—all the ticket said was, "The horse and rider sponsored by Miss Maggie." He had bought them for half price with his first day's pay since no one thought she could field a horse and rider at this late date.

"I swear I'll have your guts for garters if you bet against yourself and throw the race," Maggie said. She looked stern, and Slocum believed her. She had not only survived in Scorpion Bend, but had prospered. That meant she had a steel core to her that wasn't immediately obvious.

"That's not my way," was all Slocum said. This seemed to satisfy Miss Maggie more than carrying on about how honest he was.

"Be ready at eight o'clock sharp. I don't want to see your ugly face in my saloon or any other. Sober."

"And you'll do your best to be sure other riders are drunk as lords?" Slocum suggested. All he got for an answer was a knowing smile. Miss Maggie lifted her skirts and left. He heard a locking bar fall into place and the dull *click* of a strong iron lock to hold it in place. If he wanted to get out of the rickety barn he could, but there was no reason.

He spent some time with the horse. Getting to know

its quirks and letting it get to know him occupied more than an hour. Then Slocum pitched his bedroll next to the pawing stallion's stall and lay down to go to sleep. The hotel had a softer bed, but he wanted Black Velvet to get used to him being around. Somehow, sleep eluded him as he thought about Rachel Decker and the race and the fortune he might win . . . and Rachel Decker.

"Ready, Slocum?" Miss Maggie asked.

He held back the powerful horse as Black Velvet tried to crow-hop on him. So much energy and raw power had to be released soon.

"Ready as I'll get," he said, looking around. He had shown up at the starting line fifteen minutes before eight. The sun was just creeping over the tall mountains to the east, but it wasn't the shifting shadow and light that spooked his horse. It was the army of riders all around.

"Eighty-nine," Miss Maggie told him. "We got a real race going this time. That's danged near nine thousand dollars in entry fees in the pot, and we're still counting how many tickets we've sold."

Slocum touched his shirt pocket where the five tickets rested. He had bought them cheap, but tickets on other riders were going for ten bucks apiece. From the size of the crowd, that might add another ten thousand dollars to the grand prize. But the real money would come in laying bets.

As Slocum had done. He had put another day's pay—twenty-five dollars—on himself to finish in the top ten. He had wrangled twenty-to-one odds, so he stood to make five hundred dollars for this day's ride.

If he finished in the top ten.

"Riders," bellowed a portly man dressed in a morning coat and a tall, battered, silk stovepipe hat. "Git yer asses to the startin' line! On yer mark, git set, go!" He fired a black-powder pistol into the air, causing a huge cloud of white smoke to drift down the street into Slocum's face.

Slocum coughed and bent low, then urged his horse forward.

Half the field of riders had galloped off. The rest were playing it smart. The race was slated to last all morning and half the afternoon. A race of endurance required Slocum to have his horse as rested as possible for a strong finish. There was no way he could outrun the field with a dead-out gallop now.

He varied the pace, as did several other riders, putting on a burst of speed, then letting the horse slow to a trot to rest, then picking up the pace again, and finally dropping back to a walk. Slocum was pleased with the strength of his stallion and how well it obeyed his commands. Seeing the other horses at a breakneck gallop made the stallion want to run too, but Black Velvet obeyed when he held it back. There would be time for the real run, Slocum knew.

By the time he reached the mouth of the canyon where Mormon Will had been killed, almost a quarter of the riders had dropped out. The heat wore down on him, but his horse remained strong. As he edged into the canyon and passed the spot where the sniper had taken out both horse and rider a few days earlier, Slocum felt himself growing nervous. Only when he passed the ambush site did he feel easier, as if he unconsciously thought the sniper might repeat his cowardly attack.

But if the killer was Quinn, he rode far ahead, maybe even leading the pack of racers. That didn't mean some of his henchmen might not try to kill the opposition.

Slocum found himself keeping pace with another rider wearing a tan duster, a black Stetson turning brown with dust, and a faded red bandanna pulled up so only a pair of squinting eyes peered out. Slocum sped up, and so did the other rider. He slowed, and so did the other rider. Slocum would have worried more, except they were passing other riders as they or their mounts flagged in the crushing heat.

He had to smile as he realized that the other rider was duplicating his pace because it worked. There would be time to leave the tan-duster-clad rider behind—at the finish line.

The chasm cut through the rock widened, and Slocum saw a stretch of soothing green, cool meadow opening in front. The relief from the heat almost made him fall from his horse. He had gotten used to the heat, and any relief came as a hammer blow to his face and body. Along the way across the meadow, men cheered with yellow ribbons tied around their arms.

They were judges making sure that the riders actually completed the grueling course. There would be an army of young men at the turn, no one group quite trusting anyone else when it came to staying on course.

"Hey, you Miss Maggie's rider?" shouted one man. "You kin water over there." He pointed in the direction of an incline leading to what might be a stream hidden from sight by the steep slope. Slocum hesitated.

Another shouted, "Don't go listenin' to him. Thass nuthin' but alkali water down there. Keep going another mile. Water at the river."

Slocum wasn't sure who to believe—if either of them spoke the truth. He wished he had been able to ride the course a few times to check for such vital resources as shade and fresh water. The desert bag slung over his saddle would provide him with plenty of cool water, but his stallion was starting to flag from exhaustion. A little rest, a little water, a chance for him to wash his face, and they both would be as good as gold again.

But where to stop?

"Down the hill. Hurry or you'll lose time."

"No, no, straight on. Don't let that son of a buck gull you!"

Slocum had gained a quarter mile on the rider in the tan duster. Now it was time to let the other rider carry the weight. Slocum didn't know who it was, but most all the favored riders were locals and knew where to get water.

The rider kept going, not heading down the steep incline. This matched Slocum's instincts. Going down a slope strewn with loose stones and rocks the size of his fist, even to find decent water, seemed crazy to him. He heard the howls of outrage as he kept riding. The rider ahead angled from the course. Slocum started to worry, and then his horse bolted.

It scented water. Slocum let the stallion have its head, then reined back as they flashed through a curtain of vegetation into the center of a clear-running brook. He jumped from horseback and dunked his face in the stream. He drank his fill, and then pulled Black Velvet away from the water to keep the horse from bloating.

The other rider had decided to take a rest and let his horse recover. Slocum considered doing likewise, but had been playing out various strategies in his head. Letting the other rider pace him—use his possibly superior knowledge of how to push a horse to get the maximum effort from it—could only bring them both to the finish line together.

He wanted to beat the other rider.

Slocum mounted his reluctant horse, then started it back for the course. The road turned uphill, and Slocum chose to walk rather than trot up. His caution proved effective. He passed a half-dozen other riders who had ridden their horses into the ground and were out of the race.

He glanced over his shoulder and saw the rider in the tan duster struggling up the slope behind him. Knowing he had to make a bid for the leaders soon, Slocum urged his horse on until he came to a fork in the road. He reined back. There ought to have been a couple dozen judges there to guide him in the proper direction. He had no idea which direction to ride. Slocum dropped to the ground, giving his horse a moment's rest as he studied the road for spoor.

"I'll be damned," he said. He wasn't able to tell which road from the fork the others had taken. A brisk wind blew the dirt around, drying it and making it drift like sand. Without any piles of fresh dung to use as a marker, he might as well guess and get on with it.

"Left and uphill or right and staying level?" he wondered aloud. Slocum chose the right-hand fork.

"No!" came the faint cry from behind. He saw the duster-clad rider waving at him and pointing uphill. Intuition had kept him from being stranded at the bottom of a rocky ravine once before. Now it had to keep him from being duped by another rider who wanted him to wear out his horse on the steep upward slope.

"That's right!" Slocum called. "No!" He turned and trotted his horse through a narrowing in the road—and found himself flying through the air.

For a moment, he hung suspended, his feet only a few inches off the ground. Then he was lifted into the air, heavy ropes cutting into his body from both sides. Struggle as he might, Slocum couldn't get free of the rope trap. The loops from two lariats had dropped on him when he triggered the trap. To judge from the weight pulling him upward and the force on the ropes cutting off circulation in his body, the other ends were tied to something big and mighty heavy.

He kicked futilely and gasped—and discovered another problem. Every time he exhaled, the ropes tightened on his chest. He could not inhale again. He was being suffocated. Fast.

The world spun around him in wild circles, and then turned into a black tunnel, a tunnel collapsing into a single point of light.

Just as the tunnel was about to close, Slocum felt himself falling through the air. He landed hard on the dusty ground, too weak to even stand. Like a man who has had the wind knocked out of him, Slocum gasped and tried to ignore the pain in his chest. He finally managed to turn and look back down the road.

The rider in the tan duster held a thick-bladed Bowie knife that flashed bright silver in the noonday sun. Slocum started to go for his gun, then discovered he was too weak. He dropped to his knees and pulled the ropes off. The lariats had been cut.

By a knife. By the knife in the other rider's grip.

"Thanks," Slocum gasped out, but he spoke to the other rider's back. The man in the tan duster had tried to tell him this wasn't the course. And when Slocum had fallen into a cunning trap, the man had rescued him. That wasn't what Slocum had come to expect from other riders, but he was thankful. He vowed to look up the man and buy him a drink—an entire bottle—of Miss Maggie's finest whiskey.

Struggling to his feet, Slocum sucked in air more easily now. He retrieved his horse and got back on.

"Come on, you old nag. You had a rest. It's time to go win this race."

Black Velvet snorted indignantly at being called an old nag, then trotted easily as if telling his rider how wrong he was. Slocum took the proper turn in the road this time, and pushed his valiant stallion more than he ought to have, considering how hot the day was and how tired both he and the horse were. Somehow, Slocum felt time crushing in on him, although more than half the race remained. He had to get to the turn, and verify it with enough of the judges to assure everyone in town he had reached the midway point. Then it was only a matter of endurance getting back to Scorpion Bend.

That was all, Slocum thought.

Slocum wiped dust from his face when he saw a rider coming toward him—one he recognized instantly. His hand went toward his six-shooter in its cross-draw holster and took off the leather thong holding it down.

"Slocum," shouted Cletus Quinn. "You got quite a ride ahead of you 'fore you reach halfway."

Slocum said nothing as the gunman trotted by, looking curiously fresh for such a long race. Just the climb up the steep road ought to have tuckered him out more than he looked. Then Slocum put it out of his mind. He wasn't going to finish first today. And that didn't matter. All he had to do was finish in the top ten to make his tickets worth a lot of money. He might sell them off for fifty bucks apiece and have a stake to push on. No need to keep on with this backbreaking, ball-busting race.

Slocum shook his head to clear it of cobwebs. That would never do. He had bet on himself because he figured he could win the race. To sell his tickets and then bow out would be dishonest. He had done his share of bank robbing and other thievery, but he wasn't going to cheat men who were counting on him. Or Miss Maggie. He couldn't cheat her either, when she had been so generous with her money so far.

He snorted as he rode. He didn't owe Miss Maggie a thing. She was profiting handsomely. A slow smile came to his lips. So could he. If he won the Scorpion Bend race.

Riding more slowly, Slocum was surprised not to find others coming down the hill on Quinn's heels. How had the other man gotten so far ahead of Slocum and the others?

The trail turned steep again, and Slocum had to get off and walk. When it turned into level meadow he saw a tight knot of riders ahead, arguing. He mounted and rode toward them, wondering what the trouble might be. Then he found out. His hat went sailing through the air, taken off by a rifle slug.

Ducking involuntarily, he pressed his cheek against the side of the horse's neck and galloped forward.

"You cain't make it, mister," shouted one of the riders. "None of us kin. They got us pinned down!"

Slocum saw that all the snipers in the rocks on either side of the trail wanted was to slow down the progress of the riders. They must have let a handful—like Quinn—through, trying to determine the outcome of the race through chicanery.

"Would they actually shoot us?" Slocum called. "That'd bring the law down on them. All they want is to spook us."

"They'll kill you daid," insisted one fearful rider. "You kin die for this damned race. I ain't." He wheeled about and returned the way Slocum had just come. Many of the others seemed caught on the horns of the dilemma. Join him or try to get through to the midway point.

For Slocum there wasn't a choice. He dismounted and dashed for a pile of rock near the boulders where one gunman hid. Drawing his six-gun, he made his way through the rocks until he came up behind the gunman peering down the barrel, drawing a bead on one of the riders.

"Don't pull the trigger or you're a dead man," Slocum said. "Throw the rifle away and—"

Sharp pain lanced along his shoulder blades as another of the snipers spotted him and fired. Slocum squeezed the trigger on his Colt Navy, but missed a clean kill on the gunman in front of him. The man grunted, dropped his rifle, and got away, clutching his belly. But Slocum found three other snipers working on him now. He didn't have the ammo or the weapon to fight off men armed with rifles.

"Come on! The way's open!" shouted a racer. Several of the riders galloped past, the snipers too occupied with Slocum to do much about them. Slocum got off a couple more shots, then found himself staring into a lot of emptiness. The snipers had vanished, and so had the riders. The gunmen had done their job. All they'd needed to do was chase off a few and slow down the others.

Slocum returned to his horse, which was busy cropping grass halfway across the meadow. He mounted and made his way through the draw so recently filled with flying lead. The trail wound around a little and came out on a higher meadow. At the far end were a score of men with the yellow ribbons on their arms. Some of the riders were busy making their marks on documents showing they had made it halfway, and others were also noting the time, after peering at their pocket watches. Slocum reached the group in time to see the rider wearing the tan duster wheel his horse around and start back down.

"Hey, I want to thank you!" Slocum shouted, but the rider was oblivious to anything but the race. Slocum decided that was a good course to follow since so many had gotten there ahead of him.

"How many have checked in?" Slocum asked the trio of judges bringing him some water and a stack of papers to sign.

"Yer the twenty-first one," a judge said. "You got a chance. Lemme see. Yer ridin' for Miss Maggie, ain't ya?"

Slocum signed the papers and took one with all three men's names on it to show he had been there. He hesitated when he saw the water one man held out for him. It sloshed around in a canteen and looked to be cool, but he remembered the tricks played along the course so far. These were judges, but that didn't mean the water wasn't drugged. Knocking him out halfway back to Scorpion Bend would change the odds in someone's favor. Maybe this would favor one of the judge's favorites in the race.

"See you back in town," Slocum said, ignoring the water as he mounted. He wheeled his horse and set off at a brisk pace, determined now to pass at least eleven men.

He began to worry on the way back down the road because he didn't pass anyone going in either direction. He was dead last in the race. Sixty-eight others might have dropped out before the halfway point, but all that counted was finishing in the top ten.

Keeping a sharp lookout for snipers slowed him a mite. Then he got into the winding canyon where Mormon Will had been killed. Something of the man's spirit inhabited Slocum then. He felt stronger—and his horse shared in that power and determination. Its stride lengthened, strengthened, and gave him the chance to begin pushing harder.

By the time he got out of the canyon, he figured he was fifteenth. He was fourteenth by the time he came out of the draw and sighted Scorpion Bend in the distance. A small group of riders fought for position ahead. He passed them. Eleventh. He was eleventh and there was only a mile to go into Scorpion Bend.

He gradually overtook two more riders. One was a wild-eyed cowboy he had seen the night before drinking more than was good for any two men. Somehow the man had shucked off the hangover he must be sporting, and he rode like the wind. His opponent was the rider in the tan duster.

The distance narrowed to the finish line. Slocum heard cheers of victory and cries of outrage from those whose riders had not finished. The three riders were side by side when the cowboy fumbled at his saddle, warning Slocum of what was to come. The cowboy got his lariat free and swung it at Slocum, thinking to knock him from his mount.

Slocum was more than ready for the attack. His left hand caught the rope and gave it an unexpected tug that unseated the cowboy and left him in the dust.

The small fracas cost Slocum precious time and forced his stallion to break stride. He watched the back of the duster-clad rider ahead all the way across the finish line. Then he realized it didn't matter. He had finished tenth.

He was in the race. And the tan-duster-clad rider who had come in ninth was nowhere to be seen.

4

"Go on, Slocum, give it a try. Most fun you kin have in Scorpion Bend without taking off yer trousers!" Jed slapped Slocum on the back, causing him to spill some of his beer. Slocum smiled a little at the barkeep and the gaiety swirling around him. Somehow, he wasn't able to get into the feeling of such celebration.

"You're one hell of a rider. Betcha you kin use that six-shooter of yers too," shouted a drunk patron. Somehow, the call was taken up by everyone in Miss Maggie's saloon.

Slocum let the crowd shove him to the rear of the saloon. The back tent flap had been rolled up to let some of the gentle breeze blowing down Scorpion Bend's main street enter and clear out the smoke accumulating inside. Ten feet out back a wood plank had been balanced between two stumps. A man with a glass jar looked expectant, his hand on the lid.

"You ready? Git yer bets down, gents. Mr. Slocum's gonna git down to serious shootin'!"

Slocum drew his six-shooter and spun the cylinder. He took a deep breath. The game was simple. The man released a scorpion so it ran along the plank. Slocum had to shoot it off before it either fell to the ground or made it to the far end of the plank.

"They're fast ones, Slocum. Shoot straight," said Miss Maggie, coming up from behind. She held a thick sheaf of greenbacks in her hand. Betting had started before Slocum even agreed.

"What's it worth to me?" he asked, knowing this was the way she thought. He saw no reason not to make a few dollars off it when she stood to make hundreds. Slocum licked his lips as more crumpled greenbacks were passed over to her. She might make a thousand if he had a good run against the scorpions—whatever that might be.

"A hundred dollars a scorpion. I hate the sons of bitches," Miss Maggie said with a just a hint of malice. "One killed my lover last year, and I can't forgive any of the eight-legged monstrosities."

"A hundred a scorpion," Slocum said, getting used to the idea of making more with a single shot than if he had punched cattle all summer long. Two or three scorpions would buy him a new horse and saddle. Twice that would put him on easy street, race or no race.

"Let it go!" Miss Maggie cried.

Slocum aimed and fired by pure reflex. He blasted the scorpion halfway across the plank.

"They move quicker 'n I thought they would," he said. If he had been drunk there was no way he could have ever hit the scorpion before it got to the far side of the plank.

Another went scuttling across. It took Slocum two shots before he blew it into oblivion. A cheer went up. And then Slocum had a third one to go after. He shot a hair low and blew off part of the wood, taking the scorpion with it.

"How's that count?" he asked, reloading.

"You blowed him off fair and square," declared the man with the jar of scorpions.

"Where do you get them?" asked Slocum.

"I wrangle them myself. Sometimes I have the town kids catch them for me. I pay 'em a nickel each. They think it's good fun."

Slocum shook his head. The man paid a nickel apiece and probably charged ten dollars each for this show. Slocum lifted his six-shooter and blew another scorpion off, just a fraction of a second before it jumped to the ground. The plank had turned sticky with scorpion blood, and every new one tried to avoid the puddles, making Slocum's chore all the harder as the scorpions dodged.

He got two more before missing and letting one escape to the ground. The scorpion wrangler jumped as if he'd been stuck. His boot heel came down on the escaping scorpion, crushing it into the ground. "Never let one of the bastards escape," he explained. "They learn how to get away, you kin never stop 'em again."

"Here you go, Slocum," said Miss Maggie, handing over five hundred in greenbacks. "Remember. This is just the beginning. You take care of the stallion for the race on Wednesday. Get in the top five for the final heat and you get one thousand dollars. More, if you lay a wager or two on yourself—to win." She riffled through the sheaf of bills she held. A smile curled her rouged, full lips. Then Miss Maggie turned and went back into the canvas saloon, offering drinks for everyone. Considering how much she had made betting on Slocum, she could stand the house for drinks all night long.

Slocum knew this single act of generosity would come back to Miss Maggie a dozen times over before the night was over. And she didn't even have to cheat to get it. The revelers were ready, willing, and eager to lose their money at the faro table or to buy watered whiskey by the bottle.

The offer of free liquor caused a rush past Slocum, leaving him alone. He slipped around the tent and into the street, not sure where he was headed. Other saloons

40 JAKE LOGAN

beckoned, but he wasn't in the mood. Too many people made him uneasy. He decided to go to the stable to see if the small army of men Miss Maggie had hired to look after the stallion were doing their jobs. After a few minutes talking with the stable owner and a couple of the men, Slocum knew Black Velvet was being cared for better than he could ever hope to do.

Scorpion Bend had transformed from a sleepy little town to a bustling community trying to feed and house too many people. He walked the street, easily spotting those who lived there or nearby and those who had ridden in from all around the territory for the big race.

"Big race," Slocum said, snorting in contempt at the idea. The money was good, but these people ought to see the races in Leadville or out in Stockton. He had heard a railroad magnate had bet a million dollars on a single quarter horse race lasting less than forty seconds. It wouldn't slow any of the wagering in Scorpion Bend if he told the people there that the millionaire had lost.

If anything, that would cement it in their heads that even the high and mighty could be beaten.

Slocum slowed, and then stopped to lean against a rail as he watched a man and woman coming from the general store. The man had his right arm in a sling, and the woman struggled with a heavy box, trying to load it into the back of a wagon. Slocum hurried across the street, took the edge of the box, and lifted it into the wagon.

"There," he said. "That was a load for you." For the first time he saw that he had helped Rachel Decker.

"Hello, sir," said the woman, her eyes darting from him to the man with his arm in a sling and back.

"Slocum, Miss Decker. My name's John Slocum."

"I know. Who doesn't, after your successful ride this afternoon? And you *did* introduce yourself earlier. I may be impoverished, but I am not forgetful."

"Thanks for your help, mister," the man suddenly said. "We got to go. Now get out of the way."

The man tried to bump Slocum, but Slocum wasn't going to be moved this easily, even by a man with a busted wing. Slocum stood his ground and the man recoiled, startled at not being able to bull his way by.

"You need to learn some manners," Slocum said. "Miss Decker is well versed. Maybe she can instruct you."

"Why, you impudent—!" shouted the man. He cocked back his left hand, then reconsidered when he saw Slocum wasn't scared and had stood his ground.

"Frank, behave yourself," Rachel said peevishly. "I'm sorry, Mr. Slocum. My brother is in some pain from an injured arm."

"I'd be pleased to help you load anything else you have from the store," Slocum said. He thought a moment, then made the rest of the offer. "It would be an honor if you'd let me help you unload, since your brother's not able."

"We can get it all out back at the farm, sis," said Frank Decker. "Don't listen to him."

"Does that 'we' include you, or are you talking about only Rachel?" asked Slocum. Fire built in Frank Decker, but he only sneered, spun, and climbed into the driver's box on the wagon. Slocum turned to Rachel and said, "The offer stands. I'd like to help you unload."

"Why, thank you, Mr. Slocum. I . . . I can use some help. Frank's arm keeps him from being much help." Rachel almost stuttered now. This took Slocum aback because she seemed a confident, determined young woman. She flashed him a tiny smile, a weak thing that died quickly. "If you would care to follow us, I would like to show my gratitude."

"How's that?" asked Slocum.

She blushed and bit her lip. "Why, supper, Mr. Slocum. Help unload and I will fix us supper."

"Done," he said, thrusting out his hand. She took it and shook like a man, her grip stronger than Slocum would have thought from looking at such a petite young woman.

He finished loading the goods she had purchased at the store, then saddled his sorrel and rode alongside the wagon on the way out to the Decker farm. It was more than ten miles outside town, and the sun was just setting when they arrived. Slocum dismounted. By the time he got to the wagon, Frank Decker had vanished.

Rachel seemed not to notice, so Slocum said nothing about the way her brother had left so quickly. He set to unloading the wagon and wrestling some of the heavier items out to the barn. He dropped a fifty-pound sack of salt near a pile of burlap bags that had once held grain for the horses. Since there wasn't any grain left, Slocum figured Rachel hadn't been able to buy more. The salt was for a small herd of milk cattle lowing in the twilight.

He turned and bumped into the woman. The lovely brunette stood in the barn door and looked flustered.

"Anything wrong?" Slocum asked.

"No, nothing that hasn't been wrong before. I thought my pa had taken a turn for the worse, but Frank's with him and he's all right."

"What happened to him?" Slocum asked. The woman took a deep breath. He couldn't help noticing her ample breasts rise and fall under her gingham dress. She was upset, but now the object of that distress shifted to her father.

"He was kicked in the head by a balky mule, and he hasn't been right since. Sometimes he seems alert and knows what's going on around him." Rachel held back tears. "Other times, he's awake but doesn't know anyone, not even me. Then, like when we left for town, he simply passes out and I don't know if he'll ever wake up again."

She clung to Slocum and buried her face in his chest. He felt hot tears welling out and turning his shirt damp. Then Rachel pushed away and tried to run. He held her until she turned back to face him. Tears caused muddy tracks down cheeks that were still dusty from the ride back from Scorpion Bend. She fought to keep from crying even more.

"It gets hard trying to go it alone," Slocum said.

"I'm not alone," she said. "There's Frank."

Slocum remained silent about that. He knew good-for-nothings when he saw them. Frank Decker was a ne'er-do-well and contributed nothing but woe to this woman.

"What else can I do, John?" Rachel asked in a small voice. "Doc Marsten says there's nothing he can do for Pa. Nothing that's not expensive. Even then, there's no promise it would work."

Slocum had seen men kicked in the head go fast—and others linger for years. He remembered one who became Virginia City's town idiot. And he had been a banker before the accident.

"How much do you need to keep the banker from foreclosing on your farm?" Slocum asked. He had five hundred dollars riding in his pocket. More. He could cash in the tickets he had bought on himself. Each of them might be worth a hundred dollars now. That would mean a full thousand Rachel could use.

"No," she said sharply. "I will not be beholden to anyone, especially a man I just met."

"Sorry," Slocum said. He knew pride and what it meant to lose it. Rachel was a prideful woman, and he wouldn't do anything to rob her of her spirit.

"You aren't at all like the others in Scorpion Bend," she said. "You have a gentlemanly streak in you."

"You're not the only one accusing me of that," Slocum said. He stared down into her brown eyes. They seemed to go wider and swim about. Rachel moved closer. Her breasts crushed against his chest, and she tipped her head back, red lips parted slightly.

"Not too much of a gentleman, I hope," she said.

He kissed her.

For a moment, he wondered if he was doing the right thing. Then there was no question about it. Rachel returned the kiss fervently. Her arms went around his neck and pulled his face down so he wouldn't pull away—as if Slocum wanted to. It had been a spell since he had seen a woman as beautiful or beguiling as Rachel Decker. He ran his hands through her hair and then let them roam down her back.

He came to the full roundness of her buttocks, and pulled her body in even harder against his. She began moving her hips in slow, grinding, deliberate movements that left nothing to his imagination. They both wanted the same thing.

"Are you sure?" he asked, breaking off the kiss for a moment. "Like you said, you just met me."

She answered with another kiss, more passionate than the first. This was all the answer he needed. His lips parted and her tongue began dancing in and out, teasing his tongue, slipping sensuously along his lips, teasing and tormenting and giving him reason to expect even more from her.

Somehow she managed to get his gunbelt off, and he hadn't noticed she was even trying. His belt came undone and so did his trousers, button by button, until his manhood leaped out.

"I thought so," she said in a husky voice. Rachel dropped to her knees and began kissing and licking. Slocum found himself shifting weight from one foot to the other as his own desires mounted to the breaking point. He ran his hands over her hair and guided her back and forth a few times until he knew he couldn't let her continue.

They both wanted more than he was going to deliver. Slocum dropped to his knees in front of her and worked to get her dress unfastened. Some hidden buttons got the better of him. He let her unfasten them rather than ripping them open. And he was glad he did. Her snowy breasts tumbled out, warm and inviting.

He bent over and licked and kissed her tender flesh as she had done to him. Slowly they shifted positions, and ended up lying side by side in the hay, hands roving endlessly, pulling and tugging and unfastening until they lay naked on their discarded clothing.

"You're so lovely," he said.

"I want you, John," she said in a husky whisper. "It's been so long, too long."

He kissed the tips of her breasts, and moved into the vee formed by her alabaster thighs. She parted her knees willingly, and he moved forward. Then he was caught between surprisingly strong legs, legs used to gripping down on a galloping horse's back. With her long legs wrapped around him, he wasn't going anywhere until they were both satisfied.

He jerked his hips forward, found the precise spot they both desired, then sank slowly into her warm, moist interior. Fully in her tightness, he paused a moment and relished the feelings moving throughout his loins. Then he started a slow back-and-forth, teasing and tormenting her with his manhood as she had done earlier to him with her mouth.

"Oh, oh," she said, making tiny trapped animal sounds. "I need this, John, I do, I—ohhh!"

He gasped as she tensed around him, clutching down with her most intimate flesh. As she relaxed the grip a little, he started moving faster and faster. Friction mounted and lit a fuse deep within his loins. Rachel gasped and moaned and thrashed about beneath him. He pushed himself up on straightened elbows and looked down into her face.

Never had he seen a woman so lovely.

He thrust harder, faster, deeper. Her legs crushed down around his waist and pulled him in with redoubled strength. Slocum tried to keep a steady movement, but desire burned too brightly within him. The age-old rhythm of a man loving a woman turned ragged as he shoved powerfully, trying to split her apart all the way to the chin with his meaty shaft.

Rachel gasped and cried out in passion. Slocum kept pumping, and then spilled his seed into her yearning interior. When he began to turn limp, he sank down and lay with the woman in his arms. For some time neither said anything.

"I promised you dinner," she said.

"I think we've already had dessert."

Rachel laughed, then pushed away from him. "You can clean up over there. The water in the barrel's clean. I'll fix some vittles." She dressed quickly. Slocum watched, a catch in his throat. It had been a long time since he had seen a filly this alluring. When Rachel Decker left, she paused at the barn door and looked back over her shoulder. A smile split her face.

"I'm glad you are such a gentleman offering to help unload the supplies," she said. "Otherwise we'd never have had this chance." Then Rachel was gone. Slocum dressed quickly, went and washed his face, and left the barn.

The instant he stepped outside he felt something was wrong. He rushed to the small cabin and opened the door. Rachel stood with a flour can in her hand and a look of pain on her face.

"Rachel, what's wrong?" Slocum asked, thinking her father might have taken a turn for the worse.

"It's Frank. He . . . he took all our money. John, I'm sure he's gone into town to get drunk. And he's taken *all our money*!" she cried.

Slocum didn't want to get involved in this—but he knew he would.

5

"Has Frank done this before?" Slocum asked, leery of getting involved in a family matter. Rachel Decker glanced over her shoulder in the direction of a thin muslin curtain pulled back a few inches. From the other side came a low moan.

"Papa," she said. "Let me tend him." The brunette hurried over and pushed aside the curtain. On the bed lay a wasted, bone-thin man whiter than a potato before it's fried. He stirred, waving a hand about weakly in front of his face.

"It's all right, Pa," Rachel said, soothing him. She got a cloth and dipped it in water, wrung it out, and then put it across his head.

"Does he have a fever?" asked Slocum.

"No, but this calms him, for some reason."

And it did. The man moaned a few more times and seemed to drift off into deep sleep. Slocum felt his ire rising. How could any man go off and leave his own father in such a condition—and steal the pitiful few dollars his sister had saved, just to go on a drunk?

"I'm sorry, John. I'm sorry I asked you to get involved in this. It's so . . . sordid." Rachel didn't cry, but Slocum saw the tears welling at the corners of her chocolate-colored eyes.

"I don't promise anything, but if I find him I'll bring him back," he said.

Rachel smiled wanly. "You make it sound as if you'll bring him back at the end of a rope, dragging him the whole way from Scorpion Bend."

"Might, if he's drunk up even one red cent of your money. How much was it?"

"I don't know for sure. Maybe thirty dollars. I'd spent a lot lately getting supplies, and some tack needed mending, and—"

"I'll fetch him back," Slocum said. He kissed her lightly on the forehead and left before she saw how really mad he was. Frank Decker had bought himself a world of hurt taking the money the way he had.

Slocum swung up on the sorrel and headed back to town, taking it easy in the darkness. Overhead he picked out the summer constellations, and was startled to see Scorpio so high in the sky. He pulled out the watch left him by his brother Robert, opened the case, and peered at the face under the glow from the Milky Way. It was much later than he had thought.

He nodded to himself. A good deal of the time had been taken up pleasurably with Rachel in the barn. But his belly began to complain, and he realized he had never gotten the meal she'd promised. Somehow, that was the least of his concerns at the moment. Going hungry was nothing new for him, though doing it with five hundred dollars in his pocket certainly was.

It seemed to take forever to get back to Scorpion Bend. The town was still kicking up its heels, drunks spilling out of the saloons and into the main street. Slocum saw a man wearing a marshal's badge hammered out of what might have been a silver Mexican peso dragging two men along by their collars. As they passed him, Slocum heard the marshal say, "No more room in the jail, boys. You got to sleep it off out back. You move your scrawny butts more 'n a yard from where I plunk you down and I swear you'll be doing time over in the Laramie prison."

Slocum heard a mumbled reply, but didn't care too much about it. He considered checking with the lawman to see if he had already arrested Frank Decker on disorderly charges. Decker struck him as the kind of man who turned into a mean drunk.

Slocum snorted as this thought crossed his mind. "Hell, the man's meaner than a cornered weasel when he's sober," he said aloud.

Dismounting, Slocum went into Miss Maggie's tent saloon and looked over the crowd. If anything, it was even more crowded inside than when he'd left after the impromptu scorpion shooting. He forced his way to the bar and motioned to Jed.

"You seen Frank Decker in here recently?" Slocum asked.

"Why you lookin' for that no-account?" asked Jed.

"You see him or not?"

"I throw him out about once a week tryin' to cadge drinks. Last time I kicked him out was the day 'fore yesterday. Ain't been around tonight, not at all. You want a beer, Slocum?"

"Thanks, no," Slocum said. He made his way to the street and started hunting through one saloon after another for Frank Decker. He had finished checking the drunks passed out in the fourth one, and was thinking Decker had not come to town, when he froze. His hand moved in the direction of his six-shooter as Cletus Quinn swaggered into the saloon. The gunman looked around, then went to the bar, missing Slocum in the crowd.

The barkeep pointed to a small door to one side. Slocum thought it probably led to the cribs where women sold themselves for two bits. Quinn opened the door and ducked through, giving Slocum just a hint of what might be back there. He saw crates stacked up and rows of small whiskey kegs—or kegs of grain alcohol waiting to have gunpowder, nitric acid, and other floor sweepings added to produce the house brand of whiskey.

More than this, Slocum saw Frank Decker sitting at a low table, a man on either side of him.

Slocum went to the door and opened it a crack so he could see and hear some of what went on in the back room.

"Go on, beat him to a bloody pulp," Quinn said.

The men flanking Decker stood, knocking over their chairs. The one on Decker's right caught him with an uppercut that brought Decker up and out of his chair. The other started pounding the man's ribs, taking care to avoid the arm in the sling, as if this might cushion some of the blows.

Slocum damned himself for getting involved in this. For two cents and a bucket of warm spit he would have let Quinn and his henchmen beat up Decker. But there was Rachel and his promise to get her brother back out to their farm.

He kicked open the door and whirled into the room, ready for anything. Cletus Quinn jumped at the sudden intrusion, his hand going for the big .44 holstered at his side.

"Any time you want, Quinn," Slocum said. "Any time you want to die, go for that hogleg."

Quinn's hand started shaking. He shook his head and held his hands out in front of him as if he meant to pray.

"Not now, not here, Slocum. What do you want, busting in on us like that?"

"Decker, get on out of here," Slocum said, ignoring Quinn and his two men. "You're in no condition to take them all on by yourself."

"Let me alone, Slocum. This is none of your concern."

"Your sister's worried about you. Get on back now. *Now!*" Slocum barked. He had been a captain in the

Confederate Army, and knew how to give an order so men moved. Frank Decker jerked as if Slocum had him on a string and pulled him away from the two men intent on beating the living daylights out of him.

"No!" Quinn said.

"As I said, you think you're man enough, then go for your six-shooter," Slocum said. "Otherwise, shut your mouth." His steely gaze backed Quinn down again. The other two looked at each other, then at their leader.

They showed no sign of wanting to tangle with Slocum either.

"You're not my keeper, Slocum. I don't have to do—" That was as far as Decker got before Slocum shoved him out the small door and into the noisy saloon. Slocum backed out, then kicked the door shut. He swung around and grabbed Decker's shirt, lifting the man up and slamming him into the wall so hard that bottles stacked along it rattled.

"Listen, you get on back home or I'll cut your heart out myself, if you even have a heart," Slocum said. "And you'd better have every last nickel you took from that flour canister."

"What are you? The family priest? Is Rachel telling you everything? I don't like it, Slocum, and I want—"

Slocum slammed him back into the wall again.

"I told you what to do. If you don't do it, I might just do like your sister suggested. I'll hogtie you, put a rope around your feet, and drag you back to the farm. I saw some mighty prickly-looking plants along the way too. Be a damn shame if I didn't happen to avoid them as I was pulling you along."

"I got a . . . a broke arm. You can't—"

For a third time Slocum shoved Frank Decker into the wall. This time his cold green eyes spoke more than any words ever could. Decker turned white and gobbled like a turkey. Slocum let him slide down, kicked the door to the back room shut as Quinn tried to come out, then turned and stalked from the saloon himself.

In the cold Wyoming night he stood under the diamond-tipped stars and wanted to kill something. Then he cooled down and headed for Miss Maggie's saloon. A drink would settle his nerves.

Miss Maggie greeted him. "Mr. Slocum, Jed said you were in a while back. Glad you decided to spend some of that money of yours on my fine whiskey." She shoved a shot glass brimming with amber liquor into his hand. He knocked it back and didn't taste it at all as it burned its way down to settle in his belly.

"Oh, my, my," she said. "I think you are plumb mad at something. Care to talk about it?"

It seemed to Slocum as if he and Miss Maggie stood in the middle of a tornado. All around whirled the wild party celebrating the day's race and the winners, but the two of them stood in a bubble of calm and quiet.

"What can you tell me about Frank Decker?" he asked. Slocum figured the woman heard everything that happened in Scorpion Bend, good and bad.

"He's a loser, Slocum. Steer clear of him. He was supposed to ride in the race, but he broke his arm in some damnfool stunt when he was drunk last week. Someone bet him he could walk along the edge of the roof on the Emporia Hotel. Frank made it—halfway."

Something about the way she spoke made Slocum curious. "How much did you win?" he asked her. The small, almost guilty smile was his answer.

"Sometimes, you're too smart for your own good, Slocum. Save it for the race. We got a good chance to go all the way, you and that mighty fine stallion." Miss Maggie pursed her lips. "Enough of this talk about the likes of Frank Decker. We haven't properly acknowledged the real champion in the race."

"Black Velvet?" Slocum asked.

"To Black Velvet!" she cried. "A drink in honor of the best damn horse in Scorpion Bend!"

Somehow, the bubble of quiet around them popped and the party rushed in. But before the crowd carried him away to buy drink after drink and to hobnob with one of the top ten racers in Scorpion Bend, Miss Maggie grabbed his arm and pulled him back so she could whisper in his ear.

"Frank hangs around with Quinn. Stay away from Frank and don't go within a country mile of Quinn. He's bad medicine."

Then Slocum found himself in a drinking contest, downing shot after shot. He saw the others around him getting drunker with every shot, but his head remained clear. A glance in the direction of the barkeep told him the reason. Jed smiled and held up the bottle he had been using for Slocum's drinks—tea with just a hint of alcohol thrown in. Jed didn't want his prize attraction getting so drunk that he passed out.

The longer Slocum was sober and appeared to drink heavily, the more drinks the crowd would buy.

By ones and twos the crowd vanished. Some passed out, and others went hunting for dance halls and female company for the night. But Jed and Miss Maggie kept working those remaining, betting and buying drinks and getting them to respond in kind. More than one reveler decided to buy the entire bar a drink, much to Jed and Miss Maggie's glee.

"Lemme buy you a drink, Slocum," mumbled one drunk. "You're Miss Maggie's favorite. Haven't seen her cotton to any fella for a year or more. Anyone who's her friend is a friend of mine," the man slurred.

Slocum let him buy an overpriced, watered-down drink, and then moved on fast. Celebrity wasn't setting well with him. It wasn't as if he had done anything.

Remembering how the rider in the tan duster had saved him, Slocum looked around, hunting for the man. He didn't see anyone who might be the rider. Asking around, he found no one really knew who the rider was. But then some riders didn't use their real names. Scanning a list posted behind the bar showing the top ten riders, Slocum realized that the only one without a full name was called Pilot. Slocum figured this might be his mysterious savior, the only racer who had stuck his neck out to save Slocum's.

Why he chose to maintain anonymity was a question Slocum didn't have time to answer. From out in the street came three quick shots. No one else in the saloon noticed, but Slocum waited for more shots. A drunk usually fired until his six-shooter was empty.

When the shots didn't come, he made his way through the crush and into the cold night air. Catty-corner from Miss Maggie's saloon rose the two-story Emporia Hotel where, according to Miss Maggie, Frank Decker had tried walking along the edge of the roof. On the balcony of the hotel were two dark figures, one leaning back against the railing and the other standing beside him. Slocum thought this tableau strange, and walked into the center of the street to get a better view. Bigger towns had gas lamps. Scorpion Bend was lucky to have coal-oil lamps in the saloons.

"Hey!" Slocum shouted when he saw what was going on. The standing man was rummaging through the other's pockets.

The thief swung around, lifted his six-gun, and fanned off three more shots at Slocum. The slugs whined past, missing by a country mile. Slocum ran to the side of the hotel and took the steps up to the second floor. The door into the hallway was locked. Slocum kicked it in and then whipped out his six-gun, ready for a fight.

He pictured what the hotel looked like from the front, and guessed which rooms might lead to the front balcony. Trying one door after another finally gained him entry when he found an unlocked door. The room beyond was empty and the window stood open. He ran to it and poked his head out, then ducked back when a shot cut through the curtain flapping outward in the night wind.

Slocum dived through the window and rolled, coming up against the railing hard enough to rattle his teeth. He had his Colt Navy ready to fire, but there was only one man left on the balcony. Slocum stood and carefully advanced.

The man's head was down and one arm was thrown over the railing, supporting his weight. Slocum grabbed a handful of shirt and pulled. The head flopped back and the body twisted, showing the arm in a sling.

Frank Decker was very dead. From what Slocum could tell, he had been shot three times at point-blank range. The killer had fired three more times at Slocum as he came across the street. Decker's six-shooter was missing from his holster. Slocum guessed this was the source of the slug that had ripped through the curtains and almost taken off the top of his head.

He looked down from the balcony, knowing the killer had to have fled this way. No one had gone past Slocum into the hotel. For all the activity in the town, nothing seemed out of place, like a man skulking along or someone paying too much attention to what Slocum was doing on the balcony. He shoved his six-shooter back into his holster, snorting in disgust.

He had to tell Rachel someone had killed her brother. This was a chore he would as soon have avoided, but it was inevitable from all he had learned about Decker. Slocum searched the man, and found his pockets empty. The thief had been up here long enough to plug Decker and go through every pocket. Whatever Decker had that the killer wanted was long gone.

Slocum returned to the room he had used to get to the balcony, thinking it might hold a clue about Decker's murderer. But if the occupant had brought any gear with him, it had already been removed. Slocum reckoned the room had been rented as a meeting place, rather than a place to sleep for the night. If it had been rented at all.

As he started into the hall to go find the night clerk, he paused and turned, looking back into the room. On the floor near the window gleamed a small silver concho. Slocum picked it up and examined it.

"Zuni," he decided. He tried to remember anyone he had seen with Indian silver work on a hat or belt, but couldn't. Putting it into his pocket, Slocum went downstairs to find the clerk asleep. It came as no surprise that the man had no idea who had been upstairs. He claimed that room had not been rented, in spite of the big crowd in town for the race.

Slocum didn't push the matter. He had a murder to report to the marshal—and Rachel Decker to tell how he had failed to keep her brother out of trouble.

6

The race was tomorrow, but Slocum had a hard time keeping that in mind. The town had turned somber, or as somber as Scorpion Bend was ever likely to get, when they turned out for Frank Decker's funeral. At first Slocum thought it was out of respect for Rachel or even her father. Then he realized it was something more.

The men were taking bets on what would happen at the actual planting.

Slocum stood beside Rachel, who bit her lower lip and held back tears. He didn't know if anyone had volunteered to stay with her father. Probably not, from the way everyone in Scorpion Bend acted. But in a small circle some distance away from the grave site, a small knot of men swapped money and whispers. Slocum wasn't sure about the nature of the betting until Cletus Quinn and a half-dozen of his henchmen showed up. They dismounted down the slope of the hill where Frank Decker was to be buried, and slowly came forward. Quinn walked as if he was already squared off against Slocum.

Slocum took a deep breath, looked out over the barren terrain, and wondered why cemeteries were always in such desolate places. Scorpion Bend had put its cemetery five miles outside town, as if the residents were worried about somber ghosts coming in and spoiling their fun. The land was dotted with clumps of sere grass and jagged rock. A steady hot summer wind blew, forcing Slocum to pull his Stetson down a bit more on his head to keep it from flying off.

But Quinn and the others moved like thistles on the wind as they came forward. They marched like a platoon of soldiers on parade. An inexorable force of nature—or so Quinn would like Slocum to believe.

Slocum considered how many shots it would take to scatter them. Two or three looked apprehensive. Take out Quinn and the others would hesitate. That would give Slocum one shot, perhaps two, and the rest would turn tail and run. He had seen it before. A strong leader who had weak followers who depended on him for their backbone.

Not that he thought Cletus Quinn was all that heroic a figure. Twice before he had faced down the man, and twice before Quinn had turned tail and run like a scalded dog. As Quinn approached, Slocum tried to place the gunman on the balcony of the Emporia Hotel, six-shooter in hand, finger on trigger, and a dead Frank Decker dangling over the railing. He tried, and failed.

It could have been any of Quinn's gang. It might even have been someone else in town. Decker had not gone out of his way to win many friends. The only thing that kept Slocum coming back to Quinn as the most likely killer was the fight in the back room of the saloon. Two of Quinn's toughs had been pounding hard on Decker for some reason. And Decker had not wanted to return to the family farm.

If he had gone back after Slocum had rescued him, Frank Decker might still be alive.

Slocum pushed that from his mind. Men like Decker always found a violent way to die. It was the way they lived; it was the way they died. He sucked in a deep breath, held it for a moment, then released it slowly. He

SLOCUM AT SCORPION BEND 59

knew it was the way he would die too, because he was always out there riding in the most dangerous territory.

"I don't want them here, John. Is there anything you can do?" asked Rachel in a low voice. The preacher man was clearing his throat, getting ready for the sermon. Slocum backed off and went to stop Quinn before he came any further up the hill.

"Miss Decker doesn't want you here, Quinn," Slocum said.

"Why not? We just come to pay our last respects," said Quinn. His tone was arrogant, boasting.

"Why not? I reckon you must have been the one who put her brother in that pine box. Then again, it might just be that you're one stupid son of a bitch," Slocum said in an even voice. Anyone watching but not hearing would think he was being polite and respectful.

"You can't say that about Clete!" cried one gunman. Slocum ignored him, keeping his eyes on Quinn. It was an old trick. One distracted him, the boss plugged him. Slocum vowed if anyone was going to die today, it would be Cletus Quinn.

"I just did," said Slocum. "Are you going to leave walking or being carried? I won't let the digger plant you on the same hill as Decker, so you might want to pick out a different spot before I put you down."

Quinn bristled, then sneered. His bravado returned, and he said arrogantly, "We'll settle this, all right, Slocum. Tomorrow. At the race. Only half will qualify for the final race—and you're not going to be one of the final five."

"Your henchmen will have to be better shots this time," Slocum said. From the way a couple of the men stiffened—and the way one reached over and touched his arm, probably where Slocum had winged him out on the trail—Slocum knew he had identified his assailants.

Slocum spun and walked back up the hill, aware that his exposed back was a great temptation for Quinn and his quick six-shooter. But he returned to the grave as the preacher finished his eulogy. Rachel dropped a windflower she had plucked from a clump at the foot of the hill onto her brother's coffin.

"I hope it's better where you are now, Frank," she said softly. "I won't let Cletus Quinn get away with this. I promise you right now, I won't!" Then she jerked her head around so she wouldn't have to watch the coffin being lowered into the grave. The undertaker and his two assistants worked fast to shovel dirt on top of Frank Decker's remains. Slocum took Rachel's elbow and led her away.

"You going to be all right? Is there someone who's going to be with you?" he asked.

"Not many folks in Scorpion Bend cottoned much to us," Rachel said. "I'll be all right. I'll sit with Pa for a spell, then—" She shrugged. Slocum didn't like the idea of letting her return to the farm alone, but he had responsibilities of his own.

"I've got to exercise Black Velvet," he said.

"Black—oh, the horse. That's a mighty fine-looking stallion, John," she said, brightening. "I could breed him and . . ." Rachel's voice trailed off, as if she caught herself rambling. Slocum was heartened that something other than her own woe would take up her thoughts. He wished Decker had still had the money he'd stolen from her in his wallet, but he had been robbed after taking three slugs in the chest.

Slocum hoped Quinn had spent the money wisely. He wanted it to be the gunman's last big spending spree.

"Go on, John. I know what I have to do also. There's so much to get done. I'll be fine, John. Really."

He let the undertaker drive Rachel back to the farm. He headed straight into town to the stable, seeing the three armed guards Miss Maggie had placed around her horse.

"Afternoon, Mr. Slocum," said the leader of the

guards. He motioned to the others to shift their rifle muzzles away from Slocum. Inside the stable he found two more men standing guard, watching each other as much as watching the horse. Slocum spent some time with Black Velvet, feeding the horse a few carrots and a lump of sugar. Then he saddled the powerful stallion and rode out.

"You want some of us to ride along?" asked the leader of the guards.

"I'll be fine. If I can't outgun 'em, I can outrun 'em," Slocum said, half joking. He rode into the main street, and was startled when a spontaneous cheer went up as he trotted from town. Slocum had never sought celebrity, but he was as close as he was likely to come—short of actually winning Scorpion Bend's big race.

He looked over his shoulder at the banner flapping in the hot afternoon wind with the crude lettering. He had laughed at the notion of any race being "the big race" as he rode into Scorpion Bend. Slocum wasn't as inclined to laugh now.

A passel of money rode along with him—and Frank Decker had been killed. Slocum wasn't sure it tied in with the race, but he thought it might. Rachel Decker probably had lost her brother because of betting on a race.

Slocum trotted Black Velvet, then cantered, and finally worked up to a full gallop. He enjoyed the feel of the powerful horse and the way the ground seem to vanish in a rush under its hooves. More than this, Slocum kept his eye out for other racers exercising their mounts. He almost laughed at the way a couple of the men worked their horses, but others were expert.

Even Quinn displayed how expert he was. He might have cheated to come in first among the ten qualifying for the next leg of the race, but Slocum saw the way Quinn and his horse became one, flowing and jumping and running. Quinn was a good rider. Slocum knew he was better. It would all come down to their horses.

62   JAKE LOGAN

Slocum thought Black Velvet was better.

Slocum walked his horse and finally dismounted, leading the black stallion to a small stream meandering through the countryside. Two others who had qualified for the race tomorrow were also watering their horses.

"It's true. I saw a horse drink so much it didn't just bloat, it flat out exploded. Bang!" The man clapped his hands together sharply. The other rider and his horse jumped at the sudden noise. Slocum's hand flashed toward his six-gun. Then he relaxed and went to talk with the other racers.

"How's your training comin' along, Slocum?" asked one.

"Not so bad. I've been hunting for the rider who finished just ahead of me. Pilot was the name I saw on the finishers' list."

"Pilot? That's the *horse's* name," one man said with a laugh. "Nobody knows the rider. What's it matter? He's gonna be out in the cold after tomorrow's race. It's gonna be me and four others."

Slocum wasn't going to get into a pissing contest with the other two men. He let Black Velvet have its fill, then pulled the horse away. Some grass under a juniper gave the horse a moment of grazing.

"So you don't know who it was riding Pilot?"

"No idea at all," admitted the second rider. He pulled his horse from the stream and mounted. "Race you back to town, Slocum?"

"Why not?"

Slocum beat him by a quarter mile.

"You whip 'em up into a bettin' frenzy, Slocum, and we can split it right down the middle, you forty percent, me sixty." Jed was dead serious as he made his offer.

"You'd do better to buy up tickets on me," Slocum said. Twice that night he had been offered as high as two hundred dollars for one of the five tickets he held on himself. The price had run up since the funeral because of the way he had backed down Cletus Quinn. Slocum didn't bother telling anyone congratulating him on the showdown that Quinn was riding a horse, not shooting a six-shooter the following morning. He stood a better chance of winning as a rider than he did as a gunfighter.

Miss Maggie took bets and gave odds so fast Slocum wondered how she ever kept up with them. Then he realized half the bets would be lost, assuming an even amount was being wagered on each rider. It slowly occurred to him that he and Quinn were emerging as the favorite riders. That made his value go up like a skyrocket.

And like a burned-out skyrocket, his fame would plummet to earth if he didn't qualify in the top five for the final race.

"You low-down, stinking reptile!" shouted a man next to Slocum. He moved from the plank that served as a bar in Miss Maggie's saloon and faced another drunken patron. Before Slocum could move, Jed was across the bar and standing between the gunman and Slocum.

"You two, stop it!" shouted Miss Maggie. "Take it outside if you want to start throwin' lead around!"

Slocum stared at Jed, amazed the man had put himself between Slocum and possible harm. As if realizing what he had done, Jed shrugged, then ducked under the bar to return to his usual position pouring liquor. This drove home to Slocum what he was worth, not as a man but as a commodity. Jed didn't know him from Adam, yet he had been willing to take a bullet if it meant Slocum would ride to victory in the morning.

This sobered Slocum. He moved away, found a chair at the side of the tent, and watched the men, arguing, betting, drinking, bragging, lying. He felt cut off from them as he never had before.

"You getting cold feet, Slocum?" asked Miss Maggie. She pulled up a chair and sat beside him.

"They'd kill each other over a bet—and the bet's on me," he said. "I don't like that."

"Fame can be a heavy burden."

"I won't be famous if I lose."

"Don't you *say* that, even if you're joking. You're a winner. I saw it in you the first time you walked in. You're going to win tomorrow."

"No need to win," Slocum pointed out. "A finish in the top five is good enough for now. Let Quinn get overconfident thinking he's the best—until the real race."

"He tried to drygulch you during the first race. And I heard about the trap."

"Who told you?" asked Slocum, startled that Miss Maggie had heard how he had been tangled up in the rope snare. If he discovered who had told the saloon owner, he would have found Pilot's rider.

"One of the judges. He filed a complaint about that no-good Clay Seaton trying to decoy you down a steep hill to an alkali watering hole. I bought a dozen more men with tickets on you. That kind of trick's not going to work if you listen to the men wearing a green ribbon along with their yellow ones."

Slocum nodded, but he wasn't agreeing with Miss Maggie as much as thinking about the rope snare and how the mysterious duster-wearing rider had saved him. Miss Maggie didn't know anything about this apparently. That meant the rider was more than a mystery—he was close-mouthed.

"I'm going to turn in," Slocum said.

"The presidential suite good enough for you?" Miss Maggie said jokingly.

"The Emporia's the best," Slocum said. "See you at the starting line in the morning." Slocum worked his way out of the saloon, and let the cool night air surround him. He sucked in a deep breath, then went to the hotel. It felt strange going into the place where Frank Decker had been killed, but it beat sleeping under the stars in a town filled with drunks shooting it up.

He went past the sleeping clerk, up the stairs, and to the back of the hotel. Slocum stared at the door leading to the room where he had burst through the night before. Then he walked on to the room Miss Maggie had rented for him. It was hardly a presidential suite, but it would do. The bed was soft and didn't have too many bedbugs in it. Slocum kicked off his boots, hung his six-gun up on the brass post at the head of the bed, and lay back, staring at the high plaster ceiling, now shrouded in shadow. He let his mind wander to all that had happened to him since coming to town. Soon enough, he slipped off to sleep.

Slocum wasn't sure what it was that brought him awake. He sat up in bed and grabbed for his Colt Navy. He looked around his room, hunting for an intruder. Nothing. Standing, he padded around the room, looking in the wardrobe and under the bed. No one.

"Getting spooked for no good reason," he said to himself. But he hesitated when he passed the door leading into the hall. Reaching out, he touched the brass doorknob. He jerked back, his fingers burned.

The hotel was on fire!

7

Wisps of greasy black smoke began curling under the door like deadly fingers seeking his throat. Slocum coughed, and knew he didn't have much time to get out of the building before it burned to the ground. Like all frontier towns, Scorpion Bend was a fire hazard waiting to level every structure to cinders. He turned and grabbed at a sheet from the bed, clutching it to his face. Slocum jumped over the bed and got to the window.

He grunted as he tried to hike up the window. It refused to budge. Smoke billowed into the room, making it hard to see—and breathe. Slocum wadded up the sheet, shoved his fist in the middle, and punched at the window. The sound of shattering glass momentarily drowned out the alarm bell from outside, summoning the volunteer fire department.

Slocum used the sheet to get the shards out of his way. He paused only long enough to grab his gunbelt and boots, then went out the window. Slocum dangled from the windowsill a second, got his feet under him, and then dropped hard to the alley alongside the hotel. Quick glances left and right showed tongues of orange flame licking outward. There was no chance of saving the Emporia Hotel.

Slocum pulled on his boots and strapped his six-shooter to his waist, then hurried to the front. A dozen half-drunk firemen argued about how best to put out the fire. They weren't going to do anything soon.

"Who's inside?" Slocum demanded of one fireman. The man cocked his head sideways and stared at Slocum as if he didn't understand. "Where's the clerk?" Slocum asked.

When he didn't get an answer, Slocum ran up the steps, flung up an arm to protect his face from the heat, then plunged into the inferno of the lobby. Flames licked at his sides, almost tickling. Then it hurt. Bad.

"Anyone still here?" he shouted over the roar of the fire. Through the blaze he saw the clerk slumped over his desk. Slocum jumped over a burning chair and got to the man's side. There wasn't time to check to see if he had died already. Slocum heaved him upright, got his shoulder under the clerk, and carried him out.

Coughing and spitting to get the burnt taste from his mouth, Slocum collapsed a dozen yards away from the conflagration. He rolled away from the clerk, who moaned and began puking out his guts.

"He'll be just fine," said a bald man with a bushy white handlebar mustache. He was dressed in a nightgown, but carried a black bag.

"You Doc Marsten?" asked Slocum.

The man's bushy eyebrows rose. "Didn't know I was so famous. Didn't even have to enter that damned race either. Don't move," the doctor said, reaching for Slocum. A stab of pain went through Slocum's scalp.

"What'd you do?" Slocum asked, flinching at the dull throb remaining after the first wave of pain.

"Here," the doctor said, holding up a smoldering sliver of wood about the thickness of an Indian arrow. "Got you in the head and you never noticed."

"I do now."

Slocum winced again when the doctor brusquely applied his tincture of iodine from a purplish glass bottle. Then the man hurried off to help others overcome by smoke. The hotel had burned to gray ashes by now, going up so fast that Slocum knew he was lucky to escape. He doubted many other customers inside had gotten away. Only luck had saved him—or his sixth sense telling him something was wrong.

"What do you reckon caused it?" Slocum asked a man with a gold badge on his fireman's hat. The man took off the hat, wiped sweat from his grimy face, and shook his head sadly.

"Cain't rightly tell, but it looks like this might be more 'n an accident."

"What?"

"As I said, cain't rightly tell. But there was a kerosene lamp all bashed up toward the rear of the hotel, right on that back wall. Or where the back wall used to be."

Slocum didn't doubt someone had burned down the Emporia. How many riders in the race were inside? Besides him? If whoever set the fire only got one or two riders, it still improved his odds of winning. Slocum didn't have to ask himself too many times what sort of man would resort to such treachery.

Cletus Quinn kept popping up as the answer. And if it wasn't him, one of his men might have taken it into his head to help out his boss with a little reduction in the field of racers. Slocum saw that only the hotel and the two adjacent stores had been burned. The rest of Scorpion Bend had been saved by the volunteer firemen's quick work, in spite of the shaky start when they'd argued over how to save the hotel.

"Sacrifice the hotel, save the town," Slocum muttered as he turned toward the stable. It made sense, even if he had been inside the hotel. As he neared the stable, a guard stepped out and confronted him, shotgun leveled.

"Where you goin'?"

"You recognize me?" Slocum said, shoving his chin

forward so his face was only inches from the man. The way the man peered nearsightedly told Slocum he had done the right thing.

"Oh, you're Slocum. I got a bet on you."

"Where are the rest of the guards Miss Maggie hired?"

"Well, it's like this," the man said.

"Out getting liquored up?" Slocum guessed.

"Somethin' like that. They left me to watch after the horse. That's a mighty fine animal, believe me. I seen the best, and this one's even better."

"I'll go in and sleep in the stable," Slocum said. His bedroll and tack were inside with his sorrel. Sleeping in the straw was better than finding some other place in Scorpion Bend to spend the night. He was drawn to Rachel Decker and her farm, but it was a long ride out and Slocum wasn't overly comfortable bothering her in the middle of the night. She was still coming to grips with her sorrow over losing her brother.

Or if she believed Slocum, maybe she was plotting her revenge on Quinn. Whatever occupied Rachel Decker's night, Slocum did not want to intrude.

"I guess that's all right," the man said. "Miss Maggie said not to let anyone in, but you're ridin' and I recognize you and—"

"Good man," Slocum said, slapping the guard on the shoulder. He saw no reason to give the man time to work up a reason not to let him inside. "I'll see that you win a fortune on your bet."

The guard grinned, showing two missing teeth. Slocum opened the stable door and aroused the horses inside. He tended his sorrel, then went to Black Velvet and spent some time gentling the powerful horse. Letting the horse get used to him, his smell, his ways, would pay off for him, Slocum realized.

Slocum got his bedroll and laid out the blanket in an empty stall next to Black Velvet. He lay down, wondering if he was just antsy or if Quinn had tried to kill him by setting fire to the hotel. In spite of what the fire chief had said, it could have been an accident. Too many drunk cowboys wandered the streets of Scorpion Bend to be absolutely certain.

Slocum drifted to sleep, familiar smells all around him. And he came awake, his hand on his six-gun, just as he had in the hotel. This time it wasn't the faint whiff of smoke that alerted him, but the soft sound of someone trying not to make any noise. Slocum heard tiny scrapes of leather against wood, creaking floorboards, the harsh breathing of a man excited about what he did.

Slocum didn't have to be told that the guard outside had somehow let the intruder sneak past him.

He rose as quiet as shadows, and moved to where he could peer around the edge of the stall. Black Velvet whinnied softly, waking up because of the intruder trying to make his way across the stable. Slocum drew his six-shooter and started to cock it, then hesitated. The sound would be louder than a clap of thunder in the silent night.

"There you are, you monster," the man coming across the stable said. "I've got some nice sugar cubes for you. Just the thing to make you run tomorrow." The laugh that accompanied this claim bordered on the evil. Slocum knew that whatever the man gave Black Velvet, it wasn't going to be good.

Slocum stood and cocked his gun. The sound was every bit as loud as he thought it would be.

"What the—?" cried the startled man. He stumbled back, eyes wide and his hand clenched around whatever he carried.

"Give me a good reason not to shoot you where you stand," Slocum said.

The man reacted instinctively, throwing sugar cubes in Slocum's direction. The sudden whiteness in the dark caused Slocum to duck, giving the man the chance to turn and run for it. Slocum banged his hand against the edge of the stall. He dropped his six-gun. Rather than fumble around in the dark for it, Slocum lit out after the fleeing man.

He tackled him just inside the stable door, bringing him down hard. The man struggled like an eel, trying to kick and claw his way to freedom. Grimly, Slocum hung on until the man weakened just a mite. Then Slocum swarmed over him, fists swinging. He wasn't sure what he was hitting. He was sure he got the man's belt buckle from the sudden burst of pain all the way up his arm. But he also connected with the man's breadbasket.

A loud *whoosh* of air leaving tortured lungs was testimony to that. Slocum pressed his momentary advantage to roll the man onto his back and hold down his shoulders using both knees in a schoolboy pin. Slocum looked down into the man's face, and read a stew of pain and fear.

"I know you," Slocum said, surprised. He had expected Quinn or one of his henchmen to come by. "You finished sixth the other day."

"What of it? I didn't cheat!"

"You were trying to poison my horse, weren't you?" To Slocum's way of thinking, this was worse than if the man had tried to bushwhack him. Many were the times when another had tried to kill Slocum, but to set out to poison a horse that couldn't fight back and trusted the sugar to be good was as bad as horse theft.

Maybe worse.

"No, no, nothing like that. It'd just slow you down. That's all."

Slocum knew a lie when he heard it, and his anger started boiling. It was good he had dropped his six-shooter in the stall. He might have shoved the barrel into this son of a bitch's mouth and pulled the trigger to stop the lying.

Slocum reached down and grabbed the man by the throat. Getting off but keeping his hold on the man's windpipe, Slocum lifted the man to his feet. He dragged the intruder back into the stable and shoved him into the pile of straw in an empty stable. Slocum knelt, fumbled about, and lifted his pistol to cover the man.

"Don't kill me, Slocum. I didn't mean nuthin' by it."

"No," Slocum said sarcastically, "you didn't mean anything by it." He aimed the Colt Navy smack at the man's head and said, "Drop those drawers of yours."

"What?" The man was shocked. "I ain't no peg boy on some cattle drive."

"Do it or die where you stand," Slocum said. His tone and the unwavering six-gun convinced the man. The man fumbled at his belt, then unbuttoned his jeans and let them drop around his ankles.

"Keep going," Slocum said. "Expose yourself."

The man turned white as a sheet, but did as he was ordered.

"What are you gonna do, Slocum?"

"Here," Slocum said, pushing a large bottle of liniment toward the man with his foot. He stepped back and trained the six-shooter on the man's private parts. "Either douse yourself real good with the liniment or I'll blow off anything left dangling."

"Let me water it down," the man begged. "Thass gonna burn like hell!"

"Do it or I start shooting. I'm a good shot too."

"I seen you and the scorpions," the man admitted. With shaking hands, he picked up the bottle. He jerked when Slocum shot the cork out of the bottle.

"All over yourself," Slocum said, taking aim again.

The man whimpered, and then cried out as he poured the fiery liquid all over his genitals. Slocum kept his gun trained on the man until the bottle was empty.

"Get out of here," Slocum said.

"I'm on fire. I'm burning up, Slocum. Do something!"

"Want me to put you out of your misery, you horse poisoner?"

"No, no," gasped the man, bent double. He hobbled past Slocum, his trousers still down around his ankles. Slocum resisted the urge to kick the man in the butt as he stumbled past. Liniment was good for bruises and muscle strains—when it was diluted with ten parts water to one of the potent liniment. Straight out of the bottle, it burned like a million ants gnawing away.

Even if the man washed his private parts off in clear water, he was going to be in a world of hurt for some time.

Slocum went back to sleep, a small smile on his lips.

He was surprised at how keyed up he was. Slocum looked at the other riders, counting silently. He saw Cletus Quinn holding court across the street, boasting and carrying on. The others clustered in a tight knot, as if they could fend off all comers that way. But Slocum only got to seven, not counting himself. He had not expected to see the man who had doused himself with liniment—at Slocum's urging—but Slocum had expected the man in the tan duster to compete. He might have been caught in the hotel fire. If so, Slocum was truly sorry.

"You gents all ready to race?" called out the starter. He fumbled to load his pistol. Slocum edged Black Velvet onto the line, wondering if this race would be different from the earlier one. He had chosen to bring along a rifle this time. His trusty Winchester would even the score with any of Quinn's bushwhacking henchmen.

If they didn't backshoot him.

Slocum knew Miss Maggie had alerted the marshal and about everyone else in town about the ambush. The chance Quinn would try the same trick twice was slim. He might even run a fair race, thinking he was better than any of the others.

A stir from back down the street made Slocum turn

and look over his shoulder. The man riding Pilot galloped along, hat pulled down and tan duster flapping like thunder behind.

"Ready, set, go!" shouted the starter. His pistol went off with a muffled pop. The man on Pilot hit the starting line at a dead run and flashed past the others. Slocum had to smile. Everyone tried different tricks to get the edge on the other riders. The man who had pulled Slocum's fat out of the fire in the last race was obviously going hell-bent for leather to win this time.

Slocum put his heels into Black Velvet's sides and let the powerful horse carry him along. In a few seconds they were outside Scorpion Bend. In a minute they were half a mile toward the rocky canyon Slocum had taken into town less than a week earlier. And then the high, stony walls rose as if to crush him. On either side, riders bumped into him. Then he bent lower and got a new burst of speed out of the powerful black stallion.

This was going to be a race to remember.

Slocum intended to be able to count himself among the top five when he thought about it in future years.

8

Heat in the canyon began to take its toll on him. Slocum reined back and slowed to a walk. He had outdistanced five riders. With the man who had sampled Slocum's liniment out, that meant Slocum only had three others ahead of him. Unfortunately, that included Quinn. The man had tried to delay the racers before using snipers. Slocum knew something else would be in store for Quinn's opponents today. A rider turning up with a bullet in the head—or back—would cause such a stir not even Quinn would be able to get out of it.

Slocum imagined Quinn dangling in the hot wind with a rope around his neck. The mental picture looked good to him, but Slocum knew he had to get through the day before he could hope to pin Frank Decker's murder on Quinn.

"Top five," Slocum said over and over as his strength ebbed fast. The day was hotter than before, and every puff of wind blowing down the rocky canyon sucked that much more energy from him. More often now, he drank deeply from the burlap desert bag dangling behind him over his saddlebags. Evaporation through the damp bag caused the water to cool, giving him much-needed moisture and a crisp taste.

But the horse suffered too, and without Black Velvet's strength Slocum could never finish the race, much less win. The only consolation he could think of was that the others were similarly handicapped by the oppressive heat.

Slocum dismounted and walked the horse, giving it a rest. As he walked along, he eyed the high rim of the canyon. Any glint of sunlight off a rifle barrel would alert him to trouble ahead. But he saw nothing through the heat shimmer. He touched his pocket and traced the silver concho he had found in the Emporia Hotel after Frank Decker's murder. The owner was still a mystery, but Slocum reckoned an examination of Quinn's gear would reveal where it had come from.

"Come on, don't slow down. Neither of us will be able to move if we actually stop." He tugged at the balky Black Velvet, and the horse reluctantly kept moving. Slocum knew if he allowed the horse to rest now, he might never convince himself to keep on.

He trudged along for a mile until his feet began to hurt. He mounted and walked Black Velvet another mile. As he topped the rise that marked the middle of the canyon, he saw Cletus Quinn about a half mile ahead. The man was working on his horse's front hoof. Slocum wondered if the horse had thrown a shoe. If so, Quinn was out of the race. But even as Slocum's spirits rose, he saw Quinn mount and ride off.

Slocum frowned. Quinn wasn't following the main canyon as he worked his way through a tumble of rocks and into a narrow gash in the canyon wall.

"A shortcut? Is that how he won the other day?" Slocum wondered. He wended his way down the switchback trail. By the time Slocum reached the place where Quinn had left the main course, he made his decision. All the rules said was that a rider had to check in with the judges out in the meadow. How the rider got there after the start was not specified.

Slocum knew the terrain ahead along the main course

and how difficult it was. Cutting even an hour off the ride would give him an edge over the other riders because Black Velvet was such a strong horse, always with enough heart left for a galloping finish.

The rock slabs rising on either side brushed Slocum's shoulders. Black Velvet started getting nervous, but Slocum kept the big stallion moving until they came out into a slightly wider gash in the canyon wall. Ahead he saw the flash of a rider vanishing around a bend. He urged his horse ahead, not sure if he ought to overtake Quinn or remain hidden until they got to the meadow with its judges.

He came to a decision. He didn't want to shoot it out with Quinn right now. He wanted to beat the man and see his face. Slocum quickly found himself turning and bending and working his way through a series of narrow rock chutes. Black Velvet grew increasingly uneasy— and Slocum was sharing his horse's opinion.

Quinn might know the path through this maze, but Slocum had to rely on his tracking ability. It might take longer finding Quinn's trail than simply winning the race by out-legging all the others. As much as he hated the idea that Quinn knew a shorter route that Slocum was unable to follow, he came to a small chamber in the rock, turned his stallion around, and threaded his way back to the main canyon.

Echoes along the canyon told him the knot of riders he had passed earlier were catching up with him.

"Come on, old boy, let's trot a while. You can do it. We've got to beat Quinn." The horse seemed to understand, and responded with a strong gait. Hot air gusted past Slocum's face, cooling him by evaporating the sweat on his forehead. The faster pace made him feel better, and seemed good for Black Velvet too.

He glanced over his shoulder and saw the group of five riders he had passed working their way down the switchback trail he had already traversed. He was a good fifteen minutes ahead. Slocum wanted to put even more distance between him and the others. Some would give up. Some horses would falter. Maybe even one or two of the riders would collapse from the heat. Three riders were ahead of him. Quinn had taken a shortcut. The man riding Pilot and wearing the duster was somewhere ahead too. And one other had managed to slip past Slocum.

He let Black Velvet canter to put some distance between him and the others. It worked. A half hour of varying the pace from canter to walk brought him to a curious sight.

A man lay flat on his back in the middle of the trail. His horse stood in the shade of the canyon wall, near a stand of junipers. Slocum looked around for any sign of a sniper. He would have heard a shot and didn't expect to find a gunman. He didn't.

Approaching cautiously, Slocum looked down. He expected to see the man with his tongue lolling, perhaps already buzzard bait. Whatever had happened, the rider wasn't obviously injured.

"You all right?" Slocum called. No response. He rode closer, looking around to be sure he wasn't getting tangled up in something he couldn't handle. As far as he could tell, he and the downed rider were alone. "Your horse throw you?"

That didn't seem likely since the horse hadn't run off. If a snake had spooked the horse, it would still be running. Besides, this was the hottest part of the day in the canyon. Any snake slithering out of its burrow would fry in minutes. Sundown and later would be the worst time for diamondback rattlers.

"You need some water?" Slocum dismounted and walked closer, Black Velvet trailing him. The man groaned, but his eyes didn't open.

"Wah-ter," the felled rider croaked out.

Slocum turned to get his desert bag. From the corner of his eye he saw sudden movement. He spun back in time to have a rock smash down on the top of his head. Slocum sat down hard, and then slumped to his right side, stunned.

"Git on outta here!" cried the man who had struck Slocum, slapping Black Velvet on the rump to get the horse to run.

Slocum heard the grating of boots on the rock nearby, and knew he had to get to his feet, to fight to stay alive. He forced his aching body to move just in time to avoid another big rock crashing down on his head. This one would have crushed his skull like a rotten melon.

"Damnation," the man grunted, picking the rock up again to bash Slocum once more.

Although he saw double, Slocum had no trouble drawing his Colt Navy and pointing it smack between the two blurred images coming after him.

"You want to die out here?" he asked in a raspy voice. "Drop the rock." He sounded more in command than he really was. But the prospect of getting a slug in his gut convinced his attacker to throw down the heavy rock.

"I didn't mean nuthin' by it, Slocum. Honest."

"You wouldn't know honest if it bit you on the ass," Slocum said, regaining his senses. His head hurt like the devil, but his vision cleared.

"I'm just tryin' to win the race," the man said. "Look, Slocum, lemme give you all the tickets I have on the other riders. Someone's gonna win and—"

"*I'm* going to win," Slocum said harshly. "Tear up all the tickets. Now!"

The man did as he was told, throwing the pieces into the vagrant breeze circling around them.

"Take off one boot," Slocum ordered.

"What? Why?"

Slocum cocked his six-shooter and said, "How many scorpions did I knock off the plank before I missed? About as many buttons as you have on your jeans?"

82　JAKE LOGAN

The man hastily pulled off one boot. Slocum picked it up, went to the man's horse, and mounted.

"The boot will be a half mile down the canyon. Your horse will be there too, if I can get mine back. And if you so much as think of trying this on any other rider, I'll kill you. I swear I will kill you even if I have to come back from the depths of Hell to do it."

Without another word, Slocum rode off. This horse was somewhat rested and made good speed, allowing him to overtake Black Velvet within a mile. He dropped the man's boot where he could find it. Trying to walk with only one boot on would fry the exposed foot and cause the man's back to ache as if he'd been out baling hay and loading it on a wagon all day long.

Slocum had his own horse back, but did not dismount at first. Instead he continued to ride the other racer's horse and let Black Velvet rest. Many was the time Slocum had ridden a hundred miles in a day switching from one horse to the other, letting one rest while he rode the other.

When the horse he rode finally began to flag, Slocum jumped over to Black Velvet and let the first horse go free. Slocum figured the man hoofing it with one boot was out of the race. That left Quinn ahead of him along the shortcut and the duster-clad rider on the main course. Slocum felt he was doing real good.

He doubted any of the five men trailing him had the horse to beat him now.

Whistling, Slocum rode along at a varying pace, and was on the ground walking alongside Black Velvet when he saw a familiar figure ahead of him. The rider in the duster, with the hat pulled low and the red bandanna up over his nose was working on Pilot's left front hoof. If the horse had thrown a shoe, the race was over.

Slocum had mixed emotions over this. He had been rescued from certain disaster by the other rider, but one less in the race improved his chance of being in the top five today.

As he trotted closer, he saw a judge with a yellow ribbon around his arm come riding up. A second ribbon, a green one, fluttered in the breeze. Slocum remembered Miss Maggie telling him that she had paid off some of the judges and they would wear green ribbons. This judge came up to the duster-wearing rider and pointed down a side canyon.

Slocum reined in as he got close enough to overhear. The judge looked up, and a broad grin split his face.

"Slocum, I was jist tellin' Pilot here that you kin cut a mile or two off the course by headin' down that canyon. Quinn's way ahead, 'bout ready to reach the halfway point in the meadow."

"I know," Slocum said. "I saw him take the shortcut back down the canyon."

"Son of a bitch. And here I thought we was the only ones cheatin'," the man said, laughing.

The other rider mounted, his horse's hoof fine from the way the horse stepped quickly and sprightly.

"You going to take this cutoff?" Slocum asked him.

"You got to," the judge said hastily. "There's a young army up the canyon intendin' to do you harm if you keep on this route. Nuthin' I kin do for it 'cept to steer you past. This is a shortcut anyway, so's you'll both be comin' out ahead." The judge looked from Pilot to Slocum. "Thass okay with you, ain't it, Slocum? Me tellin' Pilot here about the shortcut?"

"I owe him one," Slocum said. The other racer shook his head, not sure what to do but obviously skeptical. Slocum wished he could see the man's face to get a better read of what went on in his head. The bandanna was soaked with sweat. Dust caked it, making his face look like some clay pot, but he didn't take off the duster or even use the bandanna to wipe away the grit.

"Suit yourself," Slocum said, taking the shortcut

pointed out by the judge. "Miss Maggie bought me some help. The green ribbon," Slocum said, pointing, "is the sign it's all right."

He didn't look back as he made his way through the rocks to a small trail leading off at an angle. It made no never mind to him if the duster-wearing rider followed or blundered ahead into the trap. Slocum had paid back the debt he owed from the last race.

Within minutes he heard the clop-clop of hooves. He had company as he made his way deeper into the canyon. In a way he was glad. Repaying the other racer's aid from the last race was the least of it. Somehow, Slocum appreciated having someone else nearby as he made his way deeper and deeper into the canyon.

But he suddenly wished he had not lured the other rider to come along when he reached the end of a box canyon.

"Son of a bitch," he said, taking his hat off and slapping it against his leg. A cloud of dust flew up. "That judge lied to me. Miss Maggie said she'd have men out here to help, but the judge must have been bought off."

He expected a stream of cursing from the other rider for jeopardizing their chances at finishing in the top five. The time wasted getting this far was the least of the problem. Their horses would be more tired by the time they got back to the main course and got to the meadow. That might mean the difference between winning and losing today.

Five riders would have gone past them by the time they retraced their trail. But the man going by his horse's name said nothing.

"I'm sorry," Slocum said. "I reckon this will be the end of the race for us."

The other rider pointed. At first Slocum didn't see what the other did. He trotted on the heels of Pilot to the base of a narrow trail zigzagging its way up the canyon wall. Dismounting, Slocum led Black Velvet up the narrow trail, following Pilot and its rider to the canyon rim.

"I'll be damned. He wasn't steering us wrong," Slocum said, seeing the meadow with the clot of judges stretching out less than a mile off. Slocum was startled when he got a harsh laugh as an answer.

The two of them mounted and maneuvered their horses down the steep slope, then side by side trotted across the grassy meadow.

"You boys are 'bout an hour behind Quinn," said one of the judges. "Figures. He manages to get here ahead of everyone. Beatin' him on Saturday is gonna be a real chore." The judges gathered with their sheaves of paper for Slocum and Pilot to sign. Slocum tucked his copy, all signed and carrying the time of their arrival, into his pocket. He wasn't surprised that Pilot had already lit out on the return path, this time following the main course. That seemed reasonable to Slocum since he might not be lucky enough to spot a shortcut trail hidden by brush as Pilot had. Before he got out of the meadow, two more racers came stumbling up, neither of them looking as if they would make it back. Slocum touched the brim of his Stetson as he rode by, knowing he would have no trouble beating them. They were tuckered out and still had half the race to run.

The only question Slocum had was if the big race on Saturday would even have five finalists in it. Quinn would finish, using his shortcuts. Pilot was ahead of Slocum. Slocum reckoned the farthest down the roster he would finish today was third.

As he galloped past the judge sporting both yellow and green ribbons on his sleeve, the man's eyes went wide, making Slocum wonder at his surprise. Slocum thought on it as he rode, and knew he had to check with Miss Maggie, but suspected the judge had tried to sidetrack him and Pilot.

"I'll get you, Slocum. I swear, I'll kill you!" shouted the man without one boot as Slocum rode past. He still had not reached the spot where Slocum had dropped his other boot. Of the man's horse, Slocum hadn't seen hide nor hair on his way back down the canyon.

It was going to be a long walk home for the man. Somehow, Slocum felt no pity for him as he hobbled along on the one blistered, cut-up foot.

Slocum maintained a pace designed to rest Black Velvet on the way back and yet stay ahead of the other racers he had passed back in the meadow. But as he rode, Slocum grew increasingly uneasy. He was missing something. The man who had been forced to dip his wick in the liniment had never started today. Quinn and the duster-clad rider were ahead of him. Two others had reached the meadow. And he had left one man on foot.

What had happened to the other three riders? Slocum had not seen them along the way where they had dropped out of the race. They ought to have been riding with those who had followed Slocum into the meadow.

What was going on?

He put his heels to Black Velvet's flanks, urging the horse to a faster gait. This race involved as much chicanery as it did honest racing. Bought and sold judges, shortcuts, traps, poisoning horses—it was all part of Scorpion Bend's big race, and Slocum had too much riding on winning to risk not being suspicious now.

"Three of them I can't account for. Where are they?"

He began pushing Black Velvet, and got out of the mouth of the canyon, to the flats outside Scorpion Bend. His heart jumped into his throat when he saw Quinn in the distance galloping to another first-place finish. But right behind him came one of the three missing riders.

And behind *him* Pilot jockeyed for position between the two other riders. If they all finished, Slocum would end up sixth—and out of the money.

"Come on, Black Velvet, show what you've got." He bent low, and the horse responded to using the reins to whip it into a gallop.

The distance closed between him and the three riders ahead. The finish line was crowded with damned near everyone in Scorpion Bend. He heard the cheers and groans. A volley of gunshots marked the celebration starting since two had crossed the finish line—Quinn and the rider who had been ahead of Pilot and the two others. Maybe the second-place finisher had taken the same shortcut that Quinn had used. That explained why Slocum had lost him along the course.

But the other two, the ones pacing Pilot—what had they done? Slocum had seen them behind him well past the shortcut Quinn had taken. Were there other ways through the canyon Slocum knew nothing about? There was a chance of that, but in his gut he doubted it. They had cheated in some other way.

Bought-off judges, other ways of cheating, all were possible. A mountain of money went along with winning the Scorpion Bend race.

Slocum closed the distance between him and the three straining to reach the finish line. His anger boiled up as he drew even with one man. Slocum veered in front of the man, forcing him to rein back. If he hadn't, their horses would have crashed together and both would have taken a spill. But Slocum ended up the winner in the confrontation.

By forcing the other rider to break stride, he assured himself of a fifth-place finish. But this wasn't enough for him. He felt deep in his gut the other rider, the one dueling it out with Pilot, had also cheated some way.

Slocum rode up on the other side of the rider, sandwiching the man between Black Velvet and Pilot. Reaching down, Slocum grabbed for the man's six-shooter. As much out of involuntary reaction as conscious thought, the man reached to stop Slocum. As he did, Slocum grabbed the man's wrist and held on. Using his knees he guided Black Velvet away.

The man popped out of the saddle and crashed to the

ground. Slocum didn't bother to look back to see if he was alive or dead. It didn't matter. If the man made a fuss about what had just happened, Slocum would make sure the argument was settled. Permanently.

He crossed the finish line amid earsplitting cheers. A few seconds later Pilot galloped across, finishing fourth. A distant fifth was the man whose horse Slocum had bumped in the rush to reach the Scorpion Bend finish line.

Slocum reined back and was immediately surrounded by Miss Maggie's supporters. He called out to the man riding Pilot, but again, horse and rider had kept riding, vanishing down the main street.

Slocum yelped as eager hands pulled him from the saddle, and he was carried along on the shoulders of men in a wildly enthusiastic crowd. It was going to be one hell of a party. And the way he felt, a shot or two of whiskey would be the perfect way to get it going.

9

"Slocum, Slocum, Slocum!" went the chant. Slocum was bounced all around and then found himself staggering along, fighting to keep his feet under him. If he slipped in the midst of this crowd, he would be stomped into the dust in nothing flat. He careened from side to side, and then was hoisted to hard shoulders and carried along with the human tide into Miss Maggie's saloon.

The tent flaps moved sluggishly in the hot afternoon breeze, and the beer Jed poured for him went down cool and smooth. Slocum's thirst was too much for him. He drained first one mug and then another. Men wanted to buy him drinks. Women crowded in and wanted even more from him. But Miss Maggie protected him, even as she raked in the money from the bets that had been laid on him.

"Five for the race on Saturday!" she called. "And Slocum's going to win!" A loud cry went up that almost deafened Slocum. Thirst slaked for the moment, he let men buy him drinks so Jed could perform some sleight of hand pushing the drinks around on the bar, reselling them to others crowding close and trying to catch a moment of glory by being noticed by a man who had qualified for the final race, the big race, the reason Scorpion Bend even existed.

An hour later the tumult died down, and Miss Maggie and Jed worked the crowd more easily, sliding beer and whiskey out and taking bets at the same time. Slocum found himself making the rounds from one table to the next, acting like a hero and wondering why he didn't charge Miss Maggie for a percentage of all the liquor she sold.

"Slocum," she said in her gravelly voice. "Come on over and set your bones down here." She pointed to a chair beside her. The small, round, beer-stained table was her private domain that none intruded upon. Slocum gratefully sat. His feet hurt, his body ached, and he wanted to curl up for an afternoon siesta. But there was something more he wanted.

"I did it," he said. "I made the cut for the final five racers."

"Here," she said, pushing a newspaper-wrapped packet across the table toward him. He took it, ripped open a corner, and saw the greenbacks inside. "A thousand, like I promised."

"What's a ticket on me worth now?" he asked. He thought of the five tickets riding high in his shirt pocket that he had paid a total of twenty-five dollars for. Simply making it into the top ten had pushed their value to a hundred dollars. What might he get for them now?

"The pot's got about ten thousand dollars in it," she said. "What with the entry fees and the money paid for the tickets tossed in, might be a tad more. Minus my cut to administer such a princely sum, of course."

"Of course," Slocum said dryly. Ten thousand dollars was a whale of a lot of money for whoever held a winning ticket. The pot would be divided up among all those holding a ticket on Slocum. If only ten tickets had been sold before the first race, he would walk away with five thousand dollars. If no other tickets had been sold, he would get the entire amount.

If he won.

If he lost, the tickets were worthless.

"You might get upward of a thousand dollars for each ticket right now," Miss Maggie told him. "I count a total of twenty tickets sold on you, but no one knows who holds them. Might be one fellow, might be twenty different men." She eyed him shrewdly.

He held five. That meant fifteen others were out there. His share would be only one quarter of the total. Still, twenty-five hundred dollars was nothing to sniff at. Slocum started working through the possibilities in his head. Sell three, get three thousand dollars right away, keep two and maybe make another thousand. If he won. If he won . . .

If he won, it was better to keep as many of his own tickets as possible. But if he lost, it was better to take the money now.

"Feeling confident?" she asked.

"The race will be rigged, and I'm not sure I know all the different ways I can lose," he said.

"My men will be out there to guarantee a fair race, as much as they can. I won't cheat, but I won't let anyone else cheat—including Quinn."

"He took a shortcut through the mountains," Slocum said. "He got in and out before I could follow the main course to the meadow. I reckon the fellow who rode to second place did the same since I didn't see him for most of the race."

Miss Maggie looked thoughtful.

Slocum went on. "And that green-ribbon-wearing judge of yours tried to sidetrack me. He sent me down a box canyon."

"What!" Miss Maggie's eyes went wide. "Describe the varmint."

Slocum did.

"That's Barr, all right. The son of a bitch sold me out! He took money from Quinn or somebody else to waylay you. I'll feed him his own ears for this!"

Miss Maggie quieted and cocked her head to one side. She studied Slocum and then asked, "How'd you end up in third place with such a detour slowing you down?"

"Pilot," Slocum said. "This is the second time Pilot saved me from looking like a complete fool. He showed me a rim trail that led right down into the meadow. I'm not sure we made it any faster, but we didn't lose any time either."

Miss Maggie chewed on this for a spell, then said, "Pilot's the long shot in the race. Wish I knew more about him."

"Jed said Pilot was the horse's name and nobody knows who the rider is."

"That's right," Miss Maggie said. "We've had some winners who refused to give anything more than a registration number. Wouldn't even mention what they called their horse, much less themselves." She shrugged. "Here in Scorpion Bend we don't much care about names and the like. All we care about is a whacking good race."

"So you don't know anything about Pilot's rider?"

"Not a thing, other than he surely can ride. I watched you and the other two crossing the flats outside of town. Pilot was galloping to beat the band, and the rider was hanging on like an expert. You and Pilot are about the best in the race. You thinking he's the one to beat and not Quinn?"

"Quinn will do whatever it takes to win," Slocum said. "Tell me about the other two in the race on Saturday."

"Don't know them either. Bloomington is the one you bumped and forced to break stride. Zachary finished just a hair behind Quinn. You reckon Zachary and Quinn are in cahoots?"

"Zachary might just be good at following a winner. That won't do him on Saturday, will it?"

"Different course then. Everyone wants to see more of what's going on during the race. Saturday, you'll go from one side of the valley to the far rim of the bowl the town sets in; then you'll circle around and finish where you started. Course, there's probably cutoffs I don't know about. The canyons in these hills likely will provide a whole passel of shortcuts."

Slocum pictured it in his head. Scorpion Bend sat in a shallow bowl of a valley. Race through to the far side, ride a half circle, and then back into Scorpion Bend. It wasn't as long a race, but folks with binoculars and spyglasses could watch more of the race—and bet on every turn along the course. Miss Maggie stood to make a fortune, if the race went her way.

Slocum vowed that it would. He wanted to win so bad he could taste it. The prize money would be good, but beating Cletus Quinn would make it even sweeter. Best of all would be seeing Quinn swinging at the end of a hangman's rope.

"I don't think Bloomington will be any trouble," Slocum said. "I don't know how he cheated, but if every citizen in Scorpion Bend can see the race, he's not going to stand a chance. Zachary might be another matter. And Pilot," he said, thinking about the duster-clad rider. "He's real competition."

"Don't forget Quinn. He's a vicious sidewinder," Miss Maggie said. "Won't stop at anything to trot across that finish line first." She heaved to her feet and went to greet a new group of revelers and relieve them of the burden of carrying so much money. Slocum sipped at his beer. The taste turned bitter on his tongue now, and he knew he had drunk enough. Outside, the sun slid down over the brim of mountains and the heat faded away like some bad memory.

"Slocum," said a well-dressed man, sliding quickly

into the chair Miss Maggie had just vacated. "I want a word with you."

"How can I help you?" Slocum asked. He had seen the man around. He thought he might be a gambler, though he didn't look like one. More of a prosperous rancher than a gambler, Slocum thought.

The next words out of the man's mouth proved he was no gambler.

"I like to win. The best way of doing that is to make an offer," the man said softly, barely audible over the hubbub in the saloon. "A thousand dollars now and another two thousand after the race."

"What?" Slocum sat up straighter.

"I'm offering you three thousand dollars to just . . . not ride as fast as you might want to otherwise," the man said. "It's worth it to me, and I can make it worthwhile for you."

"More than the three thousand?" asked Slocum.

"I'll let you know before the race who to bet on. You can pull in another pile doing that. I—" The man gasped and twitched, trying to stand but not finding the strength. Miss Maggie stood behind him, her strong fingers digging into the back of his neck. Slocum knew from the way she pinched down that she had found all the right nerves to give the man an excruciating jolt if he tried to struggle. And if he didn't, she was cutting off the flow of blood to his head.

"I ought to kill you and leave your corpse out in the sun for the ants and buzzards," Miss Maggie said, furious. "I ought to, but that would be too quick. I want you to suffer. You're trying to fix the race, aren't you, Ludwig?"

"Maggie, I—" Ludwig flopped about like a fish out of water as she squeezed down even harder.

"Get on out of here, Slocum. I got some intimate comments to exchange with Mr. Ludwig." She fixed Slocum with a steely glare. "Don't let this happen again. We got a deal. You play fair with me, and I'll make it worth your while. Cross me and you'll wish you'd been caught by Apaches and staked out in the sun."

"I don't go back on my word," Slocum said, leaving. He felt better getting outside and into the night. Up here in the Wyoming mountains wasn't like being in the desert, where it cooled off fast and left a man chilled to the bone minutes after sunset. Here the heat lingered, but not for long. Already a wind whipped down from the upper slopes and cooled overheated tempers. All along the main street drunken revelers staggered about, laughing and singing, trading bottles and lies.

Slocum felt out of place. He might be one of Scorpion Bend's current heroes, but he didn't fit in. Men thought he could be bribed into throwing the race. Others in the race tried to lead him astray, rope him, shoot him, bash him in the head with rocks. The only rider who had shown him a whit of consideration went by his horse's name, hiding his identity.

"Who are you, Pilot? On the run from the law? The town marshal's not likely to know or care who you are." Slocum had enough wanted posters riding around on his head, and not just from the problems he had run into down south in Colorado.

After the war, he had returned to the family farm in Calhoun County, Georgia. His parents were dead, his brother had died during Pickett's Charge, and he'd spent a goodly length of time recuperating from his own wounds. One day a carpetbagger judge came out and claimed no taxes had been paid during the war. Slocum knew the man fancied Slocum's Stand for his own. When the judge and his hired gunman came back to seize the land for nonpayment of the so-called taxes, Slocum rode out soon after—leaving behind a pair of new graves.

Killing a judge, even a crooked one, was a crime that was never forgotten by the law. Slocum had dodged that wanted poster for years, and feared it more than any run-in with the law he might have had in Colorado. Or Texas or Arizona or anywhere else. He had led quite a life so far.

Winning the Scorpion Bend race would be a pleasant addition to all he had done so far.

Slocum hunted around for Quinn, but didn't find the man. He thought he saw Bloomington, drunker than a lord, in a saloon down the street from Miss Maggie's, but he couldn't be sure. Slocum wanted to observe from the shadows and not deal with men trying to bribe him or women fawning over him.

At least, not any of the women in Scorpion Bend. Slocum went to the stable and saw Miss Maggie had posted a full dozen guards around Black Velvet now. The guard from the prior night was gone, replaced by men more alert and presumably more honest—they would stay bought. Slocum checked Black Velvet, saw the stallion got only the best of care, then saddled his sorrel and rode from town.

He tried to convince himself he was simply out riding, going nowhere, but somehow he ended up at the Decker farm.

It was dark except for a single light in the cabin. Cows lowed in the distance, and Slocum thought he heard a horse or two kicking at their stalls in the barn. Or the mule that had stove in the side of the elder Decker's head. Slocum didn't try to keep quiet as he rode up, dismounted, and climbed the three steps to the front door. He didn't have to knock. The door opened, and Rachel Decker was framed in the pale yellow light slipping like melted butter from inside the cabin.

"I hoped you would come, John," she said.

"I had to see how you were doing, what with your brother gone and all," he said, struggling for words. These weren't the words he wanted to say to her, but they would do for the moment. "How's your pa doing?"

"I don't see any change. There might never be, not

until he...dies." She swallowed hard, then stepped back. "Where are my manners? Come in, John. Please."

"Are you sure?" he asked.

She smiled more brightly. "Yes."

He went inside, tossed his Stetson aside, and turned to speak, only to find the woman in his arms. He didn't get out a word. Her lips crushed into his. He relished the feel of the warm, willing woman in his arms—the feel of her breasts crushing against his chest, the taste of her lips against his, the scent of her hair—simply being there with Rachel Decker.

She pushed back from him, breathless. A flush had risen and turned her cheeks red. Rachel smiled almost shyly, then proved she was anything but shy by unfastening her blouse and wiggling out of the frilly undergarment she wore so she stood before him, naked to the waist. The pale yellow light from the kerosene lamp cast shadows here and there on her body that excited Slocum with their promise.

He reached out and cupped her breasts, feeling her heart pulsing through the hard nubs capping each snowy cone. Squeezing down gently caused her to sigh and move against him again. She worked frantically now to get out of her skirt and stand entirely naked before him.

"Take me, John. I want you. I know you want me."

"Yes," was all he said as he swept her up in his arms and carried her to the simple bed at the side of the room. He was aware of the curtain that separated them from her father. And then he forgot entirely when her lips touched his before working down to his throat. She unbuttoned his shirt and her kisses followed all the way down, even when she unfastened his jeans and he kicked free of them.

Her mouth thrilled him. Her hands roved over his naked body, stroking and tweaking and teasing until he was so hard he could hardly bear it any longer. And then they were side by side in her narrow bed, naked bodies sliding across each other.

"No more, John, no more teasing," she whispered hotly in his ear. She licked and nibbled at his earlobe and then repeated her demand. "I need you so. Don't deny me."

And he did not. His hands moved from the luscious globes of her breasts, lower, over the slight dome of her belly to the furred triangle nestled between her thighs. He encountered a moistness that signaled her readiness for him. His hands parted her legs enough for him to roll over and weigh her down.

He groaned softly when he felt her hands on his manhood, guiding him forward. The tip of his shaft moved along the fleecy mound of her pubes, and then he sank full length into her inner fastness. The intrusion took away both their breaths—and all control.

Slocum began thrusting, moving faster and faster. Rachel strove with him, lifting off the bed to meet his every inward thrust. Her inner muscles clamped on him to try to prevent him from withdrawing. Carnal heat built as they moved together, their passions building.

Then Slocum found it impossible to maintain an easy, smooth rhythm. Pumping furiously, he took her—and she gave as good as she got. Slocum was never sure who enjoyed the lovemaking more. It hardly mattered because neither of them had anything to complain about.

Sweating and tired, they lay in each other's arms.

"That was so nice, John," she said dreamily. "I could get used to it."

Slocum did not answer. He could too, and that bothered him.

10

Slocum returned to Scorpion Bend a little after sunup. Most of the town was sleeping off the drunken celebration of the night before, but a few stalwart citizens went about their jobs. The general store was open, as was a tobacconist next door, along with a bookshop and a bakery down the street. The saloons were eerily quiet after the ruckus in them not so long ago. Slocum's belly grumbled from lack of good food. He had missed dinner last night in favor of more than a few beers and damned near a half-bottle of whiskey.

Even diluted by Jed, that was a gallon more than Slocum was accustomed to downing, since he'd been on the run for the past few weeks. Then he had gone out to the Decker farm. After that, he hadn't thought much of food. Not until now.

He dismounted and went to a small cafe at the edge of town. Mouth-watering aromas came from inside. He tethered his sorrel and went into the small building. Unlike most in town, this was built from brick. That was an expensive building material up here in the wilds of Wyoming where timber was more plentiful than fire-baked clay.

Settling down at a table near the door, he leaned back.

Slocum had not realized how tired he was. The race had taken it out of him, and he hadn't gotten much sleep during the night. That was a pleasant enough diversion with Rachel, but running on nothing but piss and vinegar was wearing him out.

If he got too tired, he would make mistakes. Making a mistake during the race in two days would mean losing a mountain of money—or worse. He had been trapped and ambushed and lied to and diverted enough. The rules of the final race were different. With all the riders mostly in plain view of anyone in town willing to put a spyglass to their eye, cheating would be at a minimum.

He hoped. Slocum knew men like Quinn could think of endless ways of cheating. That came more easily to them than simply following the rules and winning.

A pleasant-looking woman who'd sampled too much of her own cooking came up. She wiped her hands on her apron and beamed at him.

"Mr. Slocum! What a pleasure having you for a customer. What can I get for you this fine morning?"

Celebrity. Slocum was famous in Scorpion Bend because he was one of five riders racing for more money than most of the townsfolk would see in a lifetime. He wasn't sure he liked the attention. Still, it was nice being treated respectfully by ordinary people. All too often people in a town like this looked down their noses at strangers, cowboys—or gunfighters.

He ordered steak and onions, with fried potatoes and enough coffee to float a Mississippi riverboat. Idly, he stared out into the street waiting for his food to come. And when it did, he dived in with a vengeance, reducing the meat to nothing but a well-gnawed bone in a few minutes. He had finished a corn muffin and washed it down with the last of his coffee when he saw trouble coming in from the street.

Slocum put down his coffee mug, reached across, and pulled the keeper off the hammer of his Colt. He had been riding with the hammer on an empty chamber. Five rounds ought to be enough, he thought.

"Slocum," said Cletus Quinn in a cold greeting. "I'm surprised they let a deadbeat like you in here." Louder, Quinn called to the woman back in the kitchen. "You want me to throw out this son of a bitch for you, ma'am?"

Slocum didn't hear the answer. He didn't want to involve the woman. He dropped a ten-dollar greenback on the table and stood, getting himself squared off and ready for a fracas, either bare-fisted or with a six-shooter. It didn't much matter to him.

"I can kill you here or we can go outside and I'll do it where everyone can see what a coward you are," Slocum said. "I'd prefer to do it outside. Don't want to put the lady running this restaurant to the trouble of mopping up your blood."

"You talk big, Slocum. You ready to back up that mouth of yours?"

Slocum inclined his head slightly, indicating they ought to take the dispute outside. Quinn backed away, spun fast, and walked into the street.

Slocum followed more slowly, getting himself ready for a gunfight.

"I don't know what you got against me, Quinn, other than you know I'm going to win on Saturday."

"If you started now and galloped for two solid days, you couldn't beat me off the line," Quinn said. The gunman turned and rolled his shoulders a couple times to loosen them up.

"This the only way you think you can win? By gunning down everyone else in the race? If so, I reckon we ought to get to it." Slocum turned, ready to draw.

"You two hold on. You cain't go around shootin' up *my* town!" The marshal came boiling out of the bakery, a loaf of fresh-baked bread under his arm. He fumbled for his own side arm.

"He started it, Marshal," Slocum said. "I'm willing to finish it."

"No gunfighting! Won't allow it. The city fathers tole me to keep the shootin' down during race week."

The marshal was either braver than Slocum thought, or he was too dumb to realize he'd stepped between two men ready to throw lead at each other. The marshal looked from Slocum to Quinn and then back. A vein on the side of his head pulsed visibly, and he licked at his lips as nerves robbed him of saliva.

"You gents are better at this than I am, but I'm the Scorpion Bend marshal and I cain't let you shoot it out. Think of the money bet on you boys. What'd Miss Maggie say? And even if you don't kill one another, you might end up too wounded to even ride. You willin' to give up the chance for the pot over a little dispute?"

Slocum changed his mind about the marshal. He wasn't as dumb as he looked. Of all the arguments that might work with Cletus Quinn, this one hit the bull's-eye.

"Even Zachary might beat me if I was ridin' with a bullet in my gut," Quinn allowed. His fingers drummed on the side of his holster. Slocum watched carefully for any sign the man was going to throw down on him, thinking Slocum wasn't expecting it.

"Won't be any gunplay now," Quinn said. "Unless he starts it."

"I want to see you with a rope around your neck for killing Frank Decker," Slocum said.

"What's that? You think Quinn was the one what plugged the Decker boy?" asked the marshal.

"Can't prove it," Slocum admitted, "but he's the one. I know it."

"He's blowing smoke, Marshal, that's all. Just trying to get my goat and make you distrust me."

"Hell, Quinn, I *never* trusted you," said the marshal. Seeing the gunman's angry reaction, the marshal hurriedly added, "No offense. It's jist that Scorpion Bend don't get many gunfighters through, 'cept during the race."

The marshal left, muttering about the loaf of bread he had crushed under his arm and how his wife was going to be mad at him.

Quinn stayed where he was. So did Slocum. The sun was beating down on them, but Slocum had the feeling the danger had passed. For the moment. He waited for Quinn to make a parting insult. He wasn't disappointed.

"You know what, Slocum? You gettin' all upset over Frank Decker is a real laugh."

"Why's that?"

Quinn laughed and it wasn't a pretty sound. Like a shard of broken glass cutting across Slocum's senses, the taunting cut deep. He didn't pretend to know what was ever in another man's head, but this time he thought he did.

"Decker's the one what shot at you during the race. And you winged him. Why else would he have that sling for his arm?"

Slocum considered this. Decker was about the right size and Slocum had not gotten a good look at the man trying to ambush him. It could have been Frank Decker. Then he knew Quinn was lying. Rachel had said her brother had had his arm in the sling before Slocum even blew into town. And Miss Maggie had mentioned Frank's stunt on the roof of the Emporia Hotel, which had caused him to break his arm. No, all Quinn wanted was to sow discord.

"If he worked for you, why're you telling me this?" Slocum asked.

"I hired the son of a bitch, and he tried to double-cross me."

"That why you murdered him?"

Quinn sneered. "What do you think, Slocum? I might

be countin' him as a notch on my six-shooter, and then again, might not."

"The only reason you wouldn't is because you shot him in the chest and not in the back like the rest of the men you've left for dead." Slocum was ready for Quinn to throw down on him. The man's hand twitched, and he started for his six-gun, then stopped. The light in his eyes grew out of fear—and knowing he could never outdraw John Slocum.

"I'll beat you Saturday, Slocum. Wait and see."

"And I'll see you in your grave. The only race you'll win will be straight to Hell," Slocum promised. He watched as Quinn did an about-face and stalked off. Quinn seemed to know Slocum wasn't a backshooter like he was, though the temptation was great for Slocum. If Decker had been killed because he had done something Quinn didn't cotton to, that was almost reason enough to backshoot him.

Slocum waited until Quinn vanished down the street, turning left and stalking into a saloon. If the gunman thought putting a burr like Frank Decker under Slocum's saddle blanket meant anything when it came to the race, he was wrong. If anything, it made Slocum all the more determined not to lose to Cletus Quinn.

At the moment, Slocum didn't care if Zachary, Bloomington, and Pilot all finished ahead of him as long as he beat out Quinn.

He had started toward the stable when a familiar voice rang out. "You showed good sense, Slocum."

He turned and saw Miss Maggie sitting in a wood chair on the boardwalk in front of the tobacconist's shop. He blinked when he saw Jed come out from the store, a sawed-off scattergun resting in the crook of his arm.

"Would you have cut him down if he'd tried to shoot me?" Slocum asked.

"I got an investment to protect, Slocum," Miss Maggie said. "Jed does too. We stand to get real rich, maybe rich enough to blow this town and head for San Francisco, and you're the ticket. I don't want no low-down snake in the grass like Quinn punching the ticket before I can cash it."

"Your loyalty is so touching," Slocum said sarcastically.

"Don't get me wrong, John," Miss Maggie said, coming over to him. "I *like* you. I really do, but there's liking and then there's business. Business right now is a whole lot bigger." She smiled, and Slocum returned the grin. They understood one another, and Slocum found himself liking Miss Maggie more all the time.

"Buy you a drink?" he asked. Slocum tipped his head back and tried to estimate the time. It was hardly nine o'clock. Scorpion Bend was beginning to stir from its drunken stupor. It was a mite early for him to knock back a shot or two of whiskey, but he felt like it.

"Coffee, Slocum, coffee," Miss Maggie insisted. "I don't want you getting such a hangover you won't be able to get the best out of Black Velvet. Only two days 'fore the race, you know."

"Nobody in Scorpion Bend is likely to let me forget," Slocum said. He touched his shirt pocket where the five tickets he had bought for twenty-five dollars rested easily. Should he sell them or keep them? There was plenty of time to decide.

"The cafe where you ate breakfast has got about the best coffee. I'll buy you a cup," she said. Slocum realized the saloon owner wasn't in the habit of giving anything away. This had to be something special for her.

"You're right," she said as they sat down in the cafe. "I'm tightfisted with my money. That's why you're so special, Slocum. You can make me a mountain of money."

"There's more than that, isn't there?"

"Might be. You shouldn't ask questions you might not want answered."

"How long you been in Scorpion Bend?"

"Came here close to ten years ago. Moved up from Colorado. Before that ... well ... let's say me and the gin mills in Kansas at the end of the cattle trails were on friendly terms."

"Most folks in Scorpion Bend followed the same route," Slocum said. "That's the way the fortunes shift. What was it about this town that got it started? Silver?"

"You've got a good eye. The hills were filthy with silver ore. For maybe a year. Railroad passed us by and most folks left. A few tried their hand at ranching and farming and ... other things."

"I—" Slocum never finished his sentence. A rock crashed through the small plate-glass window, narrowly missing his head. Quick as a flash he was out of the cafe and in the street.

His six-shooter cleared leather, and he'd cocked and aimed and was about to fire when Miss Maggie shouted, "No, Slocum, don't!"

"Give me a good reason not to plug this yellow-belly," he said, Cletus Quinn in his sights.

"I got a shotgun aimed at your spine, that's why," said the marshal's frightened voice. "I don't want to get rid of two of the five racers, but I will. I seen what you done, Quinn. You pay for that window."

"I want him, Marshal," Slocum said.

"And I want a peaceful town." For a moment there was a pause and then the marshal went on, playing as much to the crowd gathering as anything else. "You two are spoiling for a fight," he said loudly enough for all to hear. "Why not do it so everyone can enjoy it?"

"Marshal, you can't do this—" Miss Maggie was shouted down by the crowd.

"We kin do it right away, Marshal!" someone shouted. "We kin put up a ring and let 'em punch each other into bloody carcasses!"

"Fifty on Slocum!" The bets went wild after that. Slocum slowly returned his six-shooter to its holster. Miss Maggie came up and clutched his arm.

"I don't want you doing this, Slocum. Even if you don't get your face punched in, your hands might be broken and you won't be able to ride."

"I'll throw the pair of you in jail for five days! Or you can duke it out!" promised the marshal.

"I'll post bail," Maggie said. "Don't—"

The saloon owner was shouted down again. This time the marshal said in a voice so low only Slocum and Miss Maggie heard, "You been hoggin' the gravy, Maggie. This is my chance to collect something more than the paltry thirty dollars a month the town pays me."

"Bare knuckles," Slocum said. He glared at Quinn and knew he could beat the man. "I'm game."

"John, no!"

Slocum yelped as he was carried away on the shoulders of a half-dozen men in the crowd. He was bounced around until they finally came to the far side of town where four posts had been driven into the ground. Men worked feverishly stringing rope from one to the other to form a crude ring. As his feet hit the ground again, he heard even more betting—and this time it wasn't all on him. More than one cowboy thought Cletus Quinn could take Slocum.

"I seen what he did to the Greek Giant, that fighter what came through Laramie a year back," one man said. "No one can take the kind of pounding that Quinn can dish out, not even Slocum."

New arguments started. As they raged, Slocum felt hands ripping off his shirt and taking his gun and gunbelt. He stood naked to the waist in the hot sun, already sweating. Miss Maggie had stopped trying to put a halt to the fight. She stood to one side, a grim expression on her face.

Slocum was beginning to have second thoughts about it when he saw the way Quinn moved. The man might not be much of a gunman, but he moved like a cougar, dodging and ducking, his fists shooting out with blinding speed.

"I'll be Slocum's corner man," offered Doc Marsten. The doctor dropped his bag, took out some tape, and began wrapping Slocum's fingers. Slocum knew what to do. He had been in fights before. The tape was as much to hold the flesh on his fingers as it was to take off that on his opponent's face.

In a low voice Marsten said, "He's got a weak belly. Keep after it. Don't be foolish enough to hit him in the face. If you connect with his jaw, you might knock him out and win—and you'd bust every damned finger in your hand."

"I know," Slocum said. He saw the doctor pour something over the tape crisscrossing his hand.

"Make a fist. And keep it balled up," Dr. Marsten said.

As Slocum clenched his fist, he felt the tape begin to harden as if he had brass knuckles on. Whatever Marsten had poured on turned his hand into rock.

A bell rang and Slocum stumbled into the middle of the ring. He circled, trying to keep the sun out of his eyes, but Quinn was cagey and knew all the tricks. Dirt under his shuffling feet kicked up small clouds of choking dust.

"I'm gonna kill you, Slocum."

Slocum didn't rise to the challenge. He knew the tricks. If he hesitated, if his attention drifted for just a second when Quinn taunted him, the other would strike. Slocum blocked two punches to his face. A roar went up in the crowd. The fight was on.

He circled and as a flash of light hit Quinn in the eyes, Slocum struck. Remembering what the doctor had said, Slocum ignored the opening he had to Quinn's chin as the man lifted his guard to block the glare. Slocum's left fist crashed into a rock-hard belly. His right followed. He felt the muscles give this time.

Slocum danced back, out of the range of Quinn's counter. A second attack knocked Quinn to the ground. The bell rang. The round was over.

"Lemme fight him!" screamed Quinn. "I slipped. He didn't knock me down. I slipped in the dirt!"

Slocum went back to his corner. Marsten threw water on him to cool him off. "You done good, Slocum," the doctor said. "Do it again and again. Don't hit him where there's any hard bone or you'll break your hands."

"Who's paying you, Doc?" asked Slocum. "You sound like Miss Maggie."

Doc Marsten grinned broadly. "I reckon there's some things that are pretty obvious. Now go get him."

Slocum took a few hard blows, and then saw how to get under Quinn's elbows and to his stomach. Every punch turned the other man's gut a little softer. Six rounds went by, Slocum winning four and Quinn getting in his licks in another two.

"Finish him, Slocum," said Miss Maggie. "Don't try playing with that varmint. You'll end up being hurt."

"Thanks for caring," Slocum said, but he knew she was right. He was in good condition, but he was already starting to tire. Most fights lasted a handful of seconds. A fight like this might go on all day long if the fighters were in good shape.

Slocum didn't want to outlast Quinn; he wanted to keep himself intact for the race on Saturday. Going out to the center of the ring, he moved as if he had tuckered himself out. He suckered Quinn into swinging a wild haymaker that whizzed past his head. Slocum stepped in and drove his fists repeatedly into Quinn's belly. When he heard a rush of wind from bruised lungs, Slocum knew he had him. He redoubled his efforts, aiming every shot directly at the man's breadbasket. This was the final straw. Quinn stumbled back and sat down hard, his eyes glazed.

"You got one minute to get up!" shouted the marshal. "One minute, Quinn, or you're gonna lose! Slocum will have beat you!"

Try as he might to whip up Quinn's anger, the marshal couldn't find the right words. Quinn struggled to get his legs under him, but they gave way as the bell rang.

"Slocum's the winner!" shouted Doc Marsten, rushing into the ring and shoving Slocum's arm high in the air. "All you galoots get back and give him some air!"

"Drinks are on the house!" shouted Miss Maggie. This caused a stampede in the direction of her saloon. She shot a look at Slocum that was completely undecipherable, then lit out to serve the half of Scorpion Bend that had been betting on the fight.

Slocum saw Zachary and Bloomington both help Quinn from the ring. That told him he would be riding against the three men in the race, but two of them would sacrifice themselves if they could take him out and let their boss win.

Slocum might have won the fight, but Quinn's odds in the race seemed overwhelming.

"I need to chisel off the tape," Doc Marsten whispered to him. "I don't want anyone knowing what I did. I might have to use this trick again later."

Slocum let the doctor and Jed guide him through the town to the doctor's surgery, where he took a hammer and began rapping at the tape that seemed to have turned to plaster of paris.

As the doctor worked, Slocum tried to piece together something that didn't seem right to him. Something about Miss Maggie perhaps. She had looked at him with scorn, disdain, and something more as he had fought Quinn. The look was familiar, and yet it wasn't.

Then Jed led him out of the doctor's office and put

him on display like a prize heifer in the tent saloon. Slocum drank round after round. Even knocking back the watered booze Jed supplied, he was giddy and mostly drunk by sundown.

11

Slocum ached all over, in spite of the rest he had gotten. Rolling over in the hay, he stretched and felt his shoulders knot up. Then he stood and looked around the stable. Somehow sleeping off the drunk in the stable seemed better than finding another hotel. Black Velvet was two stalls over and looking spunky. But something felt wrong, other than that he had pulled shoulder muscles during the fight with Cletus Quinn.

He strapped on his cross-draw holster and settled the Colt at his left hip, then made a quick inspection of the place. It took Slocum a few seconds to realize what was wrong.

No guards. Miss Maggie had hired a small army to guard the horse—and him. As he'd made his way around Scorpion Bend the night before, a half-dozen men armed with rifles or shotguns had trailed him like ducklings after their mama. It had made him uneasy until he had gotten so drunk he'd forgotten all about them. Men he had never met bought him drinks and bragged on how much money he had made them.

He remembered some of the night, some of the money exchanging hands, some of the faces—and Quinn's henchmen glaring at him as he went from one saloon to another.

Slocum peered outside. Clouds blanketed the sun, turning the day gray and promising rain at any time. The gray feeling communicated to him and made him even more uneasy. If he went to find something to eat, Black Velvet would be unguarded. After two legs of the Scorpion Bend race, Slocum knew how cutthroat the competition could be. With only five riders remaining, the odds of winning improved if any one racer could be eliminated. And under the rules, the horse ridden in the first two races had to be used in the third and final one. That made killing the horse equivalent to a bullet in Slocum's back.

"You gonna stand in the doorway or you gonna leave?" said a gruff voice. Slocum stepped from the stable and looked to his right. A man armed with a rifle, with bandoliers of ammo crisscrossing his chest and two six-shooters shoved butt-forward in their cavalry-style holsters, watched him from behind the water barrel. Leaning against the wall was a sawed-off double-barreled shotgun. This gent was ready to fight a small war—or one not so small.

"Where are the rest of the guards? Miss Maggie had a dozen men here last night."

"Most of them purty near died tryin' to match you drink for drink," the man said in a dour tone. "I'm it for now, at least until some of them sleep it off and get back over here. After seein' how you used your fists, and figurin' you kin use that six-shooter on your hip, there's not much reason to guard you."

"Look after the horse," Slocum said, wondering if the man could move without clanking. He had seen entire armies with fewer weapons. "I'm going to get some chow."

"Little wonder," the man said. "You damned near slept the day through."

Slocum pulled out his pocket watch and looked at it. It startled him to see it was almost 5:00. It had to be in the afternoon because too much light poured down, in spite of the clouds, for it to be early in the morning.

"Thursday," he muttered. Friday, and then Saturday morning for the race. It was coming at him like a freight train. Slocum stretched again and felt the muscles in his back protest. Walking slowly let him identify the sources of the pain and twist and turn and pull in different directions to get some mobility back. By the time he reached the cafe where he and Miss Maggie had worked on the cup of coffee before the bare-knuckles fight with Quinn, he was feeling as if he might live. By morning he would be ready to ride again.

And by Saturday morning, he would be ready to fight his weight in wildcats.

"Mr. Slocum, good to see you again. What can I get for you?" the woman said in greeting.

"Wondered if you'd even let me in after everything that happened," he said, settling into the chair by the window. The glass had been replaced already.

"For the price of a single pane of glass I've had a steady stream of men coming in to see where you and Quinn fought it out."

"Actually, it was down—" Then he realized the truth. The ring might have been at the edge of town, but the stories would build until he and Quinn fought in every single business in Scorpion Bend, if it increased sales.

Slocum shrugged, ordered, and felt worlds better when he finished. He noticed a small crowd forming outside, staring at him as he ate. It was as if they were memorizing every bite of food he took so they could tell their grandchildren about the day they saw the winner of the big race.

All Slocum had to do was win the race.

He went to pay, but the woman refused to take his money. "You keep on coming back, Mr. Slocum, and you'll advertise the restaurant more 'n the price of your meals.''

"Good food," Slocum said, rubbing his belly. "I'll be back."

"Everything's on the house after you win!" the woman said cheerfully. Slocum hoped her confidence was well placed. He tipped his hat to her and left, feeling better than he had any time during the last twenty-four hours.

Slocum headed for Miss Maggie's tent saloon, but didn't get far. The man blocking his path was short and had tried in vain to grow a beard. Being blond made the hair almost vanish on his chin, even if it had been more than a youthful wisp. Every move the man—the youth—made showed how nervous he was. That made him deadlier than Slocum liked, especially with the way the man's right hand kept making tiny jerking movements up toward the butt of his six-gun without actually drawing.

"You're in my way," Slocum said, staring coldly at the youth.

"You're nuthin' more 'n a pig wallowin' in slop. You don't have a backbone, Slocum. Come on, draw. I'll take you. I will!"

Everything about him told Slocum he had never faced down another man before.

"Did Quinn put you up to this?" Slocum asked softly.

"He's a great man! The best!" cried the blond youth. "You made him look like a danged fool yesterday. I cain't let you git by with that. Draw!"

"The marshal said he didn't want any gunplay in his town."

"You're yellow! Like I knowed all the time. I told Clete you'd never draw. I'm gonna cut you down where you stand, Slocum."

From the corner of his eye Slocum saw a crowd gathering. Nothing dealing with the five riders in the big race went unnoticed in Scorpion Bend. What worried Slocum more than having witnesses was how another of Quinn's henchmen might be hidden away on a rooftop with a rifle. He could plug Slocum and make it look like the fiery youth's doing.

Or he could plug the kid and blame it on Slocum. Either way, the marshal had to put him in jail. That would keep Slocum out of the race.

"I just had a fine meal," Slocum said. "I'd hate to get indigestion by killing you so soon after I'd eaten." A tiny chuckle went up in the crowd. This infuriated the already tense gunman.

"Draw or die!"

"Let's play a game, just for a minute," Slocum said. "After we play it we can have a fight, if you're still game."

"No, now!"

"What's another minute?" Slocum asked. "You think you're good enough to take me. You wouldn't be out here, if you didn't," he said, knowing that was probably a lie. The kid would be out here because Quinn had pumped him up and pushed him into the street.

"What are you gettin' at?" the man-boy asked suspiciously. The hairs in his scraggly beard quivered along with his chin.

"I'll stand about here and clap my hands. You draw when you want. If I clap before you can get your six-shooter between my hands, we'll shoot it out." Slocum knew the penalty for guessing wrong that the youth merely wanted to prove his manhood. If he had suggested this to Quinn, no matter the outcome, Quinn would blow a hole in his gut.

"You just want to see how fast I am," the youth declared.

"Right," said Slocum. "You're a smart one. But if you're fast enough once, why not twice?"

"Git on over here and let's dance!" the youth cried.

Slocum squared off at arm's length. He watched the

youth's watery blue eyes. When he knew the other man was drawing, he moved his hands with blinding speed. He clapped them twice before batting away the six-gun before it made it up to point at Slocum's belly.

Pale blue eyes went wide in surprise. Then the would-be gunman backed off.

"You're fast," he said in a hoarse voice.

"I'm even faster with a gun," Slocum said. There was no hint of boast or lie in his words. "If you've asked around, you know I don't miss."

"Yeah, Skinny, he shot off a full dozen scorpions the other night 'fore he missed one!" someone in the crowd shouted.

"A dozen?" argued another. "I seen it with my own eyes. It was closer to two dozen. Never seen shootin' like that. I won danged near a hunnerd dollars bettin' on Slocum!"

Slocum let the tall tales ebb and flow without correcting any of them. Each retelling of his prowess with his six-shooter made the blond youth turn a little paler.

"Just walk away and we're even. Do anything else and I'll find out if I can get four or five slugs into you before the hit the ground."

Again there was no braggadocio. Slocum spoke nothing but the straight truth.

The youth backed off, then almost ran. Slocum relaxed a mite. The kid would grow up and maybe cultivate a decent beard before doing anything this stupid again. But as long as he rode with Cletus Quinn, the youth was more likely to end up pushing up daisies in a potter's field than glaring out from a wanted poster.

The crowd's excited whispers burst into applause and cheers. Again. Slocum the hero. He let them herd him toward Miss Maggie's saloon. It took less than five minutes to get there, but word had already reached the woman. She glared at Slocum, shook her graying head, and finally said, "I do declare. You are a trial to me,

Slocum. Going up against a young buck like Skinny Grady was dangerous."

"Not that dangerous," Slocum said. "Not as dangerous as letting most of your guards slack off guarding Black Velvet."

Miss Maggie frowned. "What are you saying? I've got eight men, all armed to the teeth, out there watching that mountain of horseflesh."

"I reckon they must have been hiding," Slocum said. "The only one I saw was the folla loaded for bear."

"What do you mean?" The sharpness of her question brought Slocum up.

"He had bandoliers strung across his chest, like he was some Mexican *bandido*. Two six-guns shoved into cavalry holsters. A rifle and a shotgun."

"What'd he look like?"

Slocum thought for a minute and pictured the man, then said, "A couple inches shorter than me. Thinning red hair from the look of what poked out from under his hat. Splotchy skin, a fair man who'd been out in the sun too long."

"Jed!" bellowed Miss Maggie. "You hire anyone answering to that description?"

"Can't say I have. Maybe he got hired on to watch over someone's shift."

"I told them no one I hadn't given the okay to was supposed to get near that horse."

"He didn't try to make a move for me. He could have. I was more asleep than awake when I left the stable," Slocum said.

"Black Velvet," was all Miss Maggie said in a choked voice.

Slocum pushed his way through the crowd and ran all the way back to the stable. The tall stable doors stood open, and from inside came a commotion like trying to get a chicken into a burlap bag.

He looked around, but saw nothing of the man with

the bandoliers. Or any of the other guards Miss Maggie claimed she had stationed there. Slocum whipped out his six-shooter and pressed his back against the wall. Cautiously advancing, he chanced a quick look around the corner. His prudence paid off.

A bullet cut through the brim of his Stetson. Slocum jerked back involuntarily. He dropped into a crouch, swung around, and hunted for the gunman inside. For a moment, his usually sharp eyes failed to see the man with the rifle, and it almost cost Slocum some lost blood.

A foot-long tongue of flame licked out from the rifle muzzle. The sound of the man moving alerted Slocum. He swung around, hunting for the target behind the muzzle flash. His own six-gun fired again and again until he heard a grunt followed by a thud.

It sounded like a rifle being dropped, but Slocum wanted to be sure. He rolled over and came to a crouch inside the first stall. He had two shots left in his Colt Navy. He wanted to make them count.

"Slocum, you all right?" came Jed's cry from outside.

"Get back. You'll get plugged if you come inside," Slocum answered. He watched for any reaction from the man across the barn. He didn't see or hear anything, and that put him on his guard. There wasn't a quick, easy way out of the stable that Slocum couldn't cover.

"You need any help?" Jed called.

"Go around to the back. Watch the rear door," Slocum said, as much to get Jed and anyone with him out of his hair as to cut off retreat. He knew he had winged his assailant. How badly had the other been injured? Slocum didn't know.

Slocum tossed a nail he found on the floor in the direction of the stall where he thought the gunman hid. The clatter sounded like the peal of doom. No movement. Slocum waited another few seconds, then made his play. Walking in a crouch, he went to the next stall and then the next, where his sorrel pawed nervously at the floor, kicking up straw and knocking over a water bucket.

"You won't get out of here alive unless you give up," Slocum said. He wasn't sure he wanted the man to get out alive, even if he did surrender. It might be a little harder drilling him if he came out with his hands up—but not much. Slocum knew he faced a man intent on killing a horse. A man that low-down wouldn't be missed.

No answer.

Slocum didn't think he had killed the man. But now he had to find out for sure since the gunman wasn't going to flush easily. Slocum took the time to reload. With six rounds ready to fly, he dashed across the open area in the middle of the barn. He ducked down in an empty stall. A cold knot formed in his belly when he realized this was Black Velvet's stall. The horse was gone.

"You got to talk fast, horse thief," Slocum called. "I reckon a noose is waiting for you unless they treat horse thieves different in Scorpion Bend."

"It was all Quinn's doing," said a weak voice. "But he didn't just steal the horse." A laugh followed, meant to irritate Slocum into making a foolish move. "He's going to *sell* it to the Injuns. Imagine a great big horse like that dragging a squaw's travois. A work horse, not a race horse!"

Slocum held his temper in check, glanced up, and decided on how best to get the drop on the man. He saw the barrel of a rifle sticking out of the stall two down from him, and thought the man might be the one with the bandoliers.

"How many of the guards did you kill? Horse thief, backshooter, you fit right in Cletus Quinn's gang."

"He's gonna win the race. You can't ride if you don't have a horse, Slocum."

As the man rambled on, Slocum holstered his six-shooter, climbed on the edge of the stall, and jumped. He grabbed a beam supporting the loft and got over the edge.

Making too much noise getting up alerted the man to his intention to capture the high ground.

"Die, Slocum, die!" The man—it was the red-haired guard with the bandoliers—stumbled out of the stall and lifted his shotgun toward the loft. He opened up, both barrels blazing.

The man fumbled to eject the spent shells and reload. He never got the chance. Slocum rose, sighted, and fired. The slug caught the man just above the point where his bandoliers crossed. He stared down stupidly at the tiny red flower blossoming on his chest. Then the shotgun dropped from his hands, and he followed it to the floor.

Slocum felt no triumph at killing the man.

Black Velvet was gone. Quinn had stolen the horse, but had the man now dead on the floor told the truth about the horse being sold to Indians to use as a beast of burden?

That, as much as anything else Quinn had done, infuriated Slocum. He jumped to the ground and decided to talk with Miss Maggie about what they might do. He cared less about the race now than he did about getting Black Velvet back.

And sending Cletus Quinn to the promised land was next, after he recovered the horse.

12

"You're in a world of trouble now," Jed said, staring at the dead body of Quinn's henchman.

"Why? Who is he?" Slocum asked. "Somebody important?"

"What do you mean? That pile of cow flop?" Jed laughed derisively. "Ain't got the slightest notion who he might be. One of Quinn's followers, that's for sure."

Slocum understood then. The entire town wanted him to win. He was the outsider, the long shot, the dark horse in the race. And he suspected Miss Maggie might have put more than faith on him winning against Quinn.

"Will she lose her saloon if I don't race?"

"She'll be strung up by the entire town. Hell, they'll take turns to string her up more 'n once," Jed said. "I'm clearin' out right now 'fore anybody learns you lost Black Velvet."

"I didn't lose the horse," Slocum said angrily. "Miss Maggie was supposed to guard the horse. This galoot walked in and took out all her guards. Might have bought them off, might have killed them. It doesn't matter. They didn't do what they were paid to do."

"Don't go blamin' nobody else, Slocum. This is *your* fault. The horse's gone and so am I!"

Jed looked around, grabbed the first horse he saw, and lit out, riding hard and never looking back. Slocum watched him go, wondering if matters were as grim as the former barkeep thought. He guessed they were. Miss Maggie would lose more than she could afford. She'd probably given fantastic odds to get people to bet. If Quinn won—and she didn't seem the kind to bet on what had to have been a sure thing until Slocum showed up— she was ruined. She was always aiming for the big odds, he suspected.

"Got to hurry if I want that horse back in time for the race," Slocum said to himself. He saddled his sorrel and mounted, considering the ease of following Jed out of Scorpion Bend and even Wyoming. He had been on the run when he blew into town. There was no good reason he couldn't be on the run from the law in both Colorado and Wyoming.

And Miss Maggie.

He left the stable and headed out of town, not sure where to go. He needed information the woman could give him, but he wasn't going to tell her Black Velvet was gone. Not yet. There was plenty of time until the race. He hoped.

Slocum found himself out on the road leading to the Decker farm. He wondered if he had something hidden away in his mind or if this was only coincidence. The road was on the proper side of town. He hadn't taken a back trail or unusual route to get there. But he *had* ended up at Rachel Decker's place.

He sat in the saddle and simply stared at the cabin door. It was a pathetic place. The farmland was good enough, but without her father and brother to do the physical labor—if Frank Decker had ever done it—there was no reason for her to stay there.

"John, hello. I wasn't expecting you," she said, coming from the barn. She was dressed like a man, which surprised him. But he saw she had been working in the barn, apparently mucking stalls, and from the hay caught in her long brunette hair, she had been feeding the livestock also.

"Wasn't expecting to come out until after the race," he said.

"Come on in. But please be quiet. Pa is sleeping more natural-like than I've seen him in weeks."

"That's all right. I'm not even sure why I stopped by."

She stared at him, her brown eyes appraising. "You make it sound like you're leaving."

"Don't know. Depends on how good a tracker I am, and how much I can find out from you."

She glanced toward the barn, then back at Slocum. Rachel seemed nervous now.

"What do you mean? Are you tracking someone?"

He dismounted and sat on the second step leading up to the cabin door. Wiping sweat from his face gave him a few more seconds to consider what he wanted to ask of her—what he needed to tell her.

"I'm in a powerful lot of trouble back in Scorpion Bend," he said.

"You killed someone? That's awful, but I can hide you here and—"

"Worse," he said.

"The race. What about the race? They disqualified you? What of the others? Zachary and Bloomington and . . . Pilot?"

"Quinn stole Black Velvet. If I can't find the horse and return by race time Saturday morning, I'm disqualified. Miss Maggie can't afford to pay off all the bets, and I suspect the entire town is going to be mighty angry at the man causing that—and it's not going to be Quinn they'll be gunning for."

For several seconds, Rachel said nothing. Her lips moved as if she were reading to herself or figuring out some hard problem. She turned to Slocum and took his hands in hers.

"Four riders and it looks as if Quinn will win," she said. "I don't know for certain, but I think Zachary and Bloomington are in cahoots with him. That'd be three riders against Pilot, if you weren't in the race."

"You got money riding on Pilot?"

Rachel started to say something, then nodded quickly.

"You bet everything on Pilot so you could save your farm," Slocum said. "That wasn't too smart."

"It was all I could do, John. Frank was, well, you know how he was. And with Pa laid up the way he is, I don't want to move him." She sucked in a deep breath and let it out slowly. "I want to bury him on his own property. He worked hard to build this farm. It's not much, but it's all he has left."

"Move on," Slocum suggested. "Don't pine away on this hunk of rocky landscape."

"Move on where? With what? The little money I had left, Frank took. If I don't win, I'm broke. Broker than I am now, at any rate. I'll lose the farm and everything on it."

"Even if I'm in the race doesn't mean Quinn won't win—or that Pilot will," he said. "If I win, you're still out the money you bet, and the farm goes to the bank. I heard you and the banker talking the first night I rode into town."

"If you win, my bet might not pay off, but everyone else in town'll be broke too. Most all of them are betting on Quinn. After all, he's won two years running. If the bank gives any of them extra time to pay off what they owe, then I can get it too."

Slocum didn't want to tell her a banker would foreclose in the wink of an eye on everyone in Scorpion Bend. Every banker he had ever seen had long since exchanged his heart for a vault where he kept spare change but not a tot of benevolence.

And Slocum didn't want to face himself over why he had come out here. He considered asking her to ride away with him and to hell with the race and Miss Maggie and Scorpion Bend. He opened his mouth, then clamped it shut hard. The words didn't quite take shape.

"What is it, John?" Rachel looked nervously from him to the barn and back.

"Do you have any idea about Indians in the area?"

"They're all over here," she said, frowning. "Why do you ask?"

"I think Quinn might have sold Black Velvet to a band passing through. This one would have squaws, maybe a handful of warriors but not enough to scare him off."

"He's a coward," she agreed. Rachel frowned. Slocum studied her profile as she thought about what he had asked, and he almost asked her again to come with him. He jumped when the loud cries came from inside the cabin. Rachel jumped as if she had been stuck with a pin, and raced inside.

Slocum followed. She wrung out a towel and laid the cool cloth on her father's forehead. He subsided and soon slept again.

"Is he any better?"

"Yes, maybe, I don't know, John. I just don't." Rachel heaved a deep sigh. "I want to do more for him, but Dr. Marsten says there isn't anything I can do. Nothing he can do either."

Slocum looked at the fitfully sleeping man, and knew Rachel would never leave the farm as long as her pa lived and needed her. That was what members of a family did, care for one another. It was his curse that he didn't have anyone, certainly no one like Rachel Decker.

"A few days ago," she said suddenly. "An Arapaho band. A few women, several children, and perhaps a half-dozen old men. I didn't see any warriors. I thought they were out raiding, but I didn't get close enough to ask anyone."

"Where?" asked Slocum, knowing this was a long shot but one he had to take.

"On the far side of the farm. There's a pasture where I . . . I go," she said, strangely reticent about what she did there. "Follow the stream to the big bend and then go due north. I don't know if these are the Indians you want, but—"

"Thank you, Rachel," he said. He went to her and they kissed, perhaps too long. The longing he felt grew. Then she broke off and pushed away from him.

"I've got so much to do, John. I hope you find Black Velvet. It's such a noble horse."

"If I don't get back, bet everything on Pilot," he said. Rachel looked as if he had shot her. Her brown eyes went wide in surprise and her mouth opened. He quickly said, "I'm sorry. I know you don't have any money, especially any to bet on a long shot now." He reached into his pocket and pulled out two of the tickets he had bought on himself. He handed them to her.

"What do you want me to do with these?" she asked.

"Get into Scorpion Bend and find someone who hasn't heard about Black Velvet being stolen. Sell the tickets, get as much as you can. They ought to fetch at least a thousand each."

"But that'd be dishonest," she said, staring at what might be her salvation.

"Not if I get back in time to start the race," Slocum said.

"I'll hold the money for you," she said.

"Keep the money. Use it for medicine for your pa," he said. He wished he could tell her to use the money to buy her way free of the mortgage on the farm, but he suspected it amounted to a lot more than two thousand dollars.

"You're a generous man, John," she said in a small voice. "I'm a fool to let you ride out."

"I have to," he said. "And you have to watch after

your father." Slocum didn't trust himself to say any more. He mounted his sorrel, touched the brim of his hat in Rachel's direction, and galloped off, finding the stream she had mentioned and following it.

As he rode, something worried at the fringes of his mind. When he came to the big bend in the stream and turned north, he finally realized what it was. The soft ground had been cut up by a dozen horses' pounding hooves. Or maybe one horse traversing the stretch repeatedly.

Before Slocum could figure out why this bothered him, he came into the pasture Rachel had told him about. A smile came to his lips. He'd hoped it would be this easy. On the far side of the meadow he sighted a half-dozen tipis. This might just be the band of Arapaho Quinn had given the horse to.

He sucked in his breath and let it out slowly. Then again, the man he had gunned down in the livery stable might have been lying through his teeth. Quinn might not have given the black stallion to Indians, but kept it for himself or even shot it and left its carcass for the buzzards.

Quinn might have done any of those, but in his gut Slocum thought Quinn's henchman had told the truth because it would hurt the most. And it sounded like something that would appeal to Quinn's twisted sense of humor. As he rode to victory in the Scorpion Bend race, he would be thinking of the only horse that could beat him straining to pull some Indian's belongings from one campsite to another.

Slocum rode slowly, giving the Indians plenty of time to recognize him as posing no threat. When he came to a spot twenty yards away, Slocum stopped, hooked his leg across the saddlehorn, and pulled fixings out of his pocket to roll a smoke. He studied the camp, hunting for any sign of Black Velvet. He didn't see the horse, but that didn't mean much.

When the last of the cigarette vanished into smoke, Slocum exhaled and let the final puff escape his lungs. It was probably time to enter the camp. More than one child had stared at him for several minutes, then turned and walked away. He wouldn't be startling anyone.

Dismounting, Slocum walked into the camp. An old man, older than dirt from the way his face was lined, squinted at Slocum as if everything he saw was dimmed by time, and shuffled up.

Slocum exchanged greetings in Arapaho, which was about all he knew of their language.

"I speak some of your language," the old man said.

Slocum exchanged a few more pleasantries, although he was seething inside with need for action. To rush the conversation now would be to turn off the spigot that would pour forth what he needed to know.

He finally found the right place to slip in his request. "I see few horses in your camp," Slocum said. This caused a small stir in the Arapaho, who quickly settled back into an impassive expression.

"We have few. The ones we have are scrawny and not good."

"I look to buy a stallion, but one that is special to my people."

"Your people?" the Indian said, coming close to laughing.

"It must be a powerful stallion, a black stallion," Slocum said. "I would pay well for it."

"Look at this horse," the old brave said, motioning. Two youngsters rushed up, leading a dun horse. From the look of it, the horse was older than the Indian offering it for sale. "A good horse. It will carry you far."

"No, no, it must be black," Slocum said. He took a moment to look over the horse being held for his examination. "And a stallion, not a mare."

"This is good. It will serve you. One hundred dollars."

It was Slocum's turn to stifle a laugh. This refugee from a glue factory wouldn't bring half that from a blind man who had no idea what a horse was good for.

"A special horse. This is what I need. Do you know anyone with a black stallion? I have heard a powerful chief rides one, which is why I have come to you." Slocum had no qualm about buttering up the Indian.

"We have nothing like that," he said. One of the small children began whispering to the other. Slocum couldn't overhear what was said, but he had an idea it was exactly the information he needed.

"I give this to you as a present," Slocum said, handing the old Indian his pouch of tobacco. "And I hope you find a buyer for this noble horse." He patted the dun horse and turned to go. As if suddenly remembering, he turned, reached into his pocket, and took out lumps of sugar intended for Black Velvet. Slocum gave several cubes to each of the boys.

"For your horses," he said. He cast a sidelong glance toward the old Indian, who worked to build himself a smoke. Slocum asked in a lower voice, "Where's the black stallion? Who has it?"

"Big Stump's squaw got the horse," the boy said. "But Big Stump came back from hunting and took it for his own."

"Who gave the horse to the squaw?"

The boys fell silent. They stared at him, as if the question meant nothing.

"Who brought the horse to your camp to give to Big Stump's squaw?" he asked, trying a different way of getting the information.

"A man from your town. The one who trades for silver from the south."

Slocum reached into his pocket and pulled out the concho he had found in the room near where Frank Decker had been killed. He held it out for the boys to examine.

"He wore silver work like this?"

They agreed. "We get it from the Zuni and Hopi," one said. "We have nothing to do with the Navajo. They would kill us for our horses."

Slocum nodded toward the boys and mounted his horse. Big Stump was out on a hunt. Asking when he might return would only lead to a series of frustrating questions without decent answers. Slocum knew the hunter's return depended on how good the game was. He also knew a brave with a new horse might want to stay out longer to get used to riding it.

A horse like Black Velvet would make any brave feel like a king. Getting it away from Big Stump was going to be difficult, Slocum knew. More than that, he had to find the Indian before the race Saturday morning.

He had a lot of searching ahead of him and had no idea how he could rush it.

13

Slocum rode around the meadow with its ankle-high juicy grass, studying the ground illuminated by the bright morning sun, trying to track Big Stump, probably part of an Arapaho hunting party, through the greenery. The more he studied the bare patches of ground, the more confused he became. Along the stream leading to the meadow were dozens of hoofprints. Back and forth across the entire breadth of the pasture land were other hoofprints, as if a cavalry troop had ridden through recently. Examination showed the horses had been shod, which only made matters worse for Slocum.

He wanted to find unshod Indian ponies—except for Black Velvet, who had had new horseshoes put on a week earlier to get ready for the race. Slocum sought a mixing of metal shoe print and plain-hoofed horses, and wasn't finding it.

"Where would an Indian go hunting around here?" He had to think like an Indian or he would wander aimlessly. Slocum looked around at the tree-covered hills surrounding the grassy area, and saw no way to figure out where the Arapaho might head. He didn't even know what game the Arapaho hunted. Probably deer this time of year, but possibly bear also. If the latter, the party would go higher into the mountains, and he would have no chance of ever finding Black Velvet before the race.

"Got to believe Big Stump is nearby hunting deer or other small game," he said to himself. "Where would I go if I wanted venison for dinner? If I were out hunting for deer on a strong, new horse, where would I head?"

Slocum sat on a rock, felt as if he was missing something, then knew what it was and wished he hadn't given away his tobacco. He pulled up a stalk of grass and sucked on it while he thought. Every time he made a complete circle around the meadow he came back to one wooded area to the west. It led up into low foothills where deer might go. And something about it told Slocum this was the spot *he* would go if he wanted to ride a powerful horse and learn how to control it.

"Let's hit the trail," he said to his sorrel. The horse looked at him and canted its head to one side, as if telling him the grass here was good and why look for another horse that wasn't even his. Slocum mounted and rode at a brisk gait toward the wooded area he kept staring at. A smile came to his face when he saw the first trace of an unshod horse in a soft patch of soil.

He made his way through the woods, trying to keep to the track but losing it often. The Indian had made no effort to hide his track. The pine needles and other detritus forming a mat on the ground masked any real trail, however. Slocum finally dismounted and walked on foot, as much to avoid the low branches in juniper and other low-growing trees as to better see the trail.

He came to the far edge of the wooded area and stopped. A smile came to his lips. Echoing across the rocky, open area in front of him were pounding hoofbeats. Slocum swung into the saddle and started for it, wary of spooking an Indian hunting party. That was a good way to end up with a bullet in his head or an arrow in his back. He had crossed half the rock-strewn field when he slowed. The rider ahead had already vanished, probably working upslope. But something didn't seem right to Slocum.

Standing in the stirrups, he tried to catch sight of the hunter. Nothing. Slocum turned slowly, studying the horizon. He grew increasingly uneasy and didn't know why.

Then he found out.

The bullet and the report from the rifle both reached him about the same time. Slocum jerked to the side, got his feet out of the stirrups, and fell heavily. He moaned, then bit his lip to keep from making any more sound. Playing possum wasn't his way, but the slug had passed close enough to his head to stun him.

Carefully reaching up, he touched the bruised area where the slug had ripped past. The skin wasn't broken, but the area was tender. He had come as close to getting plugged as he could without spilling blood. But as he lay on the ground, every other ache and pain returned to him. Worst of all was the lance of flame across his shoulders where he had been creased during the first leg of the race.

If the men shooting at him got any better, he'd be dead. As it was, Slocum felt as if he already had one foot in the grave.

He lay between two foot-high rocks jutting up from the ground. Those protected him from another bullet and gave him a chance to watch for his assailant. If the Indian had bushwhacked him, the man could wait a long time. Arapaho were as patient in hunting as they were fierce in fighting.

Two men rode in from the edge of the rocky field. Neither was Arapaho. At this distance Slocum couldn't identify them, but he suspected they were Quinn's henchmen. That meant Quinn might not be too far away. Moving slowly, Slocum inched his hand down to his six-shooter and drew it. The other men had the advantage with their rifles.

He could wait. He was patient.

Slocum got off a shot that took the second rider from

the saddle. The man's head jerked back and he threw up his hands, dropped his rifle, and simply fell over the rump of his horse. The horse bolted and kicked out like a mule, catching him after he hit the ground.

Slocum didn't have to examine the body to know that that one was dead. The other swung about, not sure what was going on.

"Clay, what—?"

Slocum got up and ran hard. The crunch of his boots against the gravelly ground alerted the mounted man—too late.

Launching himself, Slocum swung his six-shooter with his right hand even as he grabbed a handful of shirt with his left. He pulled back and yanked the man off the horse.

Slocum followed him to the ground, pinning his shoulders with his foot. Cocking his six-gun, Slocum bent down and shoved it into the man's face.

"You drygulched me," he said coldly. "Any reason I shouldn't blow your head off like I did your partner's?"

"S-Slocum," the man gasped out. "Don't sh-shoot me. Don't do it."

"That's not a reason. See you in Hell." Slocum lifted his six-shooter so the man stared straight down the barrel.

"Quinn," the man gasped out. "Quinn wanted us to shoot you. Weren't our idea, no, sir, not ours! I'd never—"

"Quit lying," Slocum said "Where's Quinn?"

"He—around. I dunno where. Honest, Slocum, I don't. Me and Clay was out lookin' for somethin' to shoot for supper and—"

"So of course you took a potshot at me," Slocum said sarcastically. "Quinn. What's he doing out here?"

"He don't confide in me. I think he's just practicin' for the race tomorrow."

Slocum tried to remember the lay of the land. This valley might lie on the far side of the bowl where the people in Scorpion Bend huddled, all caught up in placing bets and hoping to win enough money to get out of their misery. The race would follow the far side of the mountain. Remembering how Quinn had found a shortcut before for the other races, Slocum wondered if cutting through to this side of the mountain, then getting back somewhere around the Decker farm, might not be a faster route.

He didn't know and that bothered him.

A moment of inattention almost did Slocum in. The man twisted away, spun on his back, and kicked out, getting Slocum on the knee. A boot toe shoved behind Slocum's ankle sent him spinning around and tumbling downhill. He didn't roll far, but it was enough to give his captive time to scramble to his feet and take off for the hills.

Slocum retrieved his six-shooter, leveled it at the fleeing man's back, and hesitated long enough to let the man escape. Slocum wasn't sure if he had done the right thing letting the man go. Quinn and all his henchmen had shown they were nothing but backshooters. But Slocum figured he could handle himself. If this man getting away proved dangerous later on, so be it.

He shoved his six-gun back into his holster and set off to retrieve his sorrel. The horse had ran to the far end of the rocky area, and shied when he approached.

"Easy, easy," he said, wishing he had the sugar cubes he had given the Arapaho boys. Truth was, Slocum wished for a lot of things he didn't have. Like Black Velvet. Like information about what was going on. Like Cletus Quinn in his gunsights.

He mounted and rode back to where the man he had shot lay sprawled on the ground. Slocum considered letting the buzzards and ants take care of him, then heaved a sigh. He took care of his own dirty work. Dismounting, Slocum spent the next twenty minutes scraping out a shallow grave and piling rocks on top of the corpse. Coyotes might nose into it, but at least there was some chance the man might rest in peace.

Which was more than he probably deserved.

Dusting off his hands, Slocum mounted again and rode in the direction taken by Quinn's other henchman. As he had feared, no tracks had been left on the rock. Slocum had to believe Quinn knew he was out prowling around, hunting for Black Velvet.

"Forget Quinn," he told himself. "Find Black Velvet. Beating Quinn in the race is more important." And it was. Miss Maggie had put more than faith in him. She had bet everything.

A sad smile came to his lips when he considered how accurate this was in Rachel Decker's case. She had bet everything, hoping to win or at least go broke in such a way that the bank didn't foreclose right away on her father's legacy.

He felt an obligation to them, and even to his own vanity. He couldn't let a scoundrel like Quinn beat him. And Quinn would, unless Slocum retrieved the horse in time for the race.

He rode toward the higher slopes, thinking this would be where he would hunt for deer. The Arapaho would be around here, he knew. All he had to do was find the hunting party and bargain for the horse. How he would do this was beyond Slocum, since he doubted any brave would swap a fine stallion like Black Velvet for any amount of white man's greenbacks.

Slocum reined back and held down a cry of pure anger when he saw a sheet of paper punched down over a twig on a limb about eye level.

He yanked it down.

The note was simple. It said: "I sold the horse for a buffalo hide."

Slocum didn't have to guess who had left the note. Quinn was around somewhere and his henchman had gotten back to rejoin the gang. That Quinn hadn't lain in ambush somewhere rather than leaving a note puzzled Slocum. For a few seconds.

Quinn might enjoy crossing the finish line tomorrow knowing he had bested Slocum more than seeing Slocum's body lying in the hot sun. Crowing about his victory, bragging to Slocum's face, lording it over the others would appeal to Quinn's egotism more than leaving a dead foe.

"He wants me to know he's better. He wants to brag to me and make me mad about it," Slocum said to himself. Even thinking this, he rode cautiously, an ear cocked to the side and both eyes studying the terrain for any hint of a trap.

Quinn and his men might be out somewhere on this side of the mountain practicing—or laying a trap for him—but Slocum found the spoor from the Arapaho hunting party before he came across Quinn.

A small area a dozen yards from a brook showed where the Indians had camped not too long back. Slocum studied the sign he found and saw he had been right. They had moved upslope, probably thinking they could find a herd of deer. He smiled when he found the tracks of one shod horse amid the unshod.

"Black Velvet," he said, looking up. His belly complained from lack of food. He drank deeply from the stream to quell the grumbling so he could ride on. Wasting time now seemed more of an obstacle to getting the stallion back than anything else. Once he had Black Velvet trotting behind him and he was in Scorpion Bend, he could sit down for a fine dinner at any of the restaurants and greatly enjoy the meal.

No horse, no enjoyment of a hot meal or anything else. He knew he might as well keep riding like Jed had already done if he didn't get back to town in time for the race.

Slocum wanted to hurry as he tracked the Indian hunting party, but the rocky ground kept him from riding hell-bent in the direction the Arapaho had taken. The trail wasn't impossible to follow, just hard. And then he came across a real dilemma.

Crossing over the hunting party's tracks were those of shod horses. He carefully outlined the hoofprints, and figured no fewer than four riders had ridden to the west while the Indians were going off at an angle, heading uphill.

"Quinn," he said. The gunman had come by after the Indian party. Slocum doubted Quinn even realized how close he had been to the Arapaho—and it might not have mattered to the man. He had his damned buffalo hide in exchange for Black Velvet.

Quinn or the Indians? Slocum wanted to even the score with Quinn, and it was a big debt he had to pay off in hot lead. But Black Velvet wasn't with Quinn. The stallion was being ridden by a warrior.

The decision came quickly. Slocum mounted and rode after the Indians. Recovering the horse was more important. With Black Velvet under him in the race, Slocum could dash Quinn's hopes and make the man eat crow.

He began to worry when the sun started slipping down faster and faster in the Wyoming sky, heading toward the mountains in the west. The hunters were moving faster than he liked, as if they had some destination in mind. Slocum knew nothing about the migratory patterns of the Arapaho. They might pass this way several times a year and have specific hunting grounds they favored.

Feeling pressured by time evaporating on him, Slocum threw caution to the wind and rode faster. He didn't even try to follow the hunting party's tracks now. He figured they were going up, and that was where he would go also.

A distant rifle shot brought Slocum around. It had come from his right—and uphill.

It was getting toward twilight, time for deer and other animals to come out and graze, drink, and otherwise make themselves seen. Realizing this might be his only chance, Slocum rode in the direction of the gunshot, hoping Big Stump sat astride Black Velvet—and that the Arapaho would be willing to give up such a fine horse to the first White Eyes who came along.

He made sure his six-shooter rode easy in his holster.

14

Another gunshot echoed through the valley, guiding Slocum toward the hunting party. He slid from the sorrel, tethered it to a limb, and made his way on foot to a place where he could spy on the Arapaho. Two braves crouched in shadow not a dozen feet from him. They were upwind and didn't scent him.

Slocum settled down to watch, waiting to catch sight of Black Velvet. The two braves suddenly leaped from cover, shouting and waving their arms. Without even realizing he did it, Slocum's hand flashed to his six-shooter and drew it. Then he relaxed a mite. The Indians weren't after him. They were flushing game.

A large buck, its antlers swishing in the air as it sized up the threat from the two Arapaho, twisted and faced them. A single shot caught the deer at the right shoulder. It took one step, fell to its knees, then spat pink froth that turned black in the twilight. With a wheezing noise the buck collapsed.

The Indians whooped in glee as they raced forward. Their knives flashed in the fading light as they set to dressing out the carcass. Slocum watched, wondering which was Big Stump. Then he knew the answer.

From the far side of the wooded area strutted a tall,

bare-chested brave, his rifle resting in the crook of his left arm—or what remained of it. The brave had lost his left arm halfway up to his elbow. That handicap hadn't stopped him from making a good shot under poor conditions. Slocum pressed a little harder into the tree giving him shelter to keep from being seen.

It would be as easy for Big Stump to drop him as a two-hundred-pound buck.

Slocum slipped away, circling in an attempt to find either the Arapaho camp or where Big Stump had tethered his horse. Black Velvet had to be close by. Slocum felt it in his bones. But he didn't find the horse by the time the Indians finished with the deer.

He sank down again and watched as they trooped off into the night. Slocum knew tracking Arapaho was risky, but he had no choice. They were a hunting party, not out on the warpath. That might save him if he made a careless move. They might be too interested in roasting a haunch of venison for their dinner than in listening for someone on their trail.

Slocum worried he was getting turned around as the Arapaho followed a game trail through the forest. Getting back to his sorrel seemed almost impossible to him by the time he smelled pungent juniper smoke. Crouching and advancing carefully, he found the Indian camp.

Two Arapaho were already roasting Big Stump's kill. Two others worked on moccasins, repairing them, and then moving on to sharpen knives and clean rifles. Big Stump sat by himself, staring into the fire. What he pondered, Slocum had no idea. From the far side of the camp came gentle whinnying, betraying the location of the Indian remuda.

The Indians started their meal. Slocum's mouth watered at the smell of roasting venison. Big Stump had made a clean kill, so the meat wouldn't taste gamy. And Slocum hadn't eaten since he couldn't remember when.

"After I ride back into Scorpion Bend on Black Velvet," he promised himself. How he was going to rescue his sorrel didn't enter his plans at the moment. He'd hate to lose the stalwart horse, but retrieving Black Velvet had to be the only thing in his mind. Too many people were counting on him being at the starting line tomorrow morning.

He paused, considering what he was about to do. Horse thieving was a worse crime than killing somebody, especially if they needed it. But Slocum wasn't stealing from the Arapaho—he was only taking back Miss Maggie's property, which Quinn had stolen. Whoever received stolen property had to expect to lose it.

"Just doing the marshal's job," Slocum said to himself. He stepped from shadow, then froze. The horses in the rope corral reared. One pawed the air, kicking in his direction. He let the animals calm down before taking another step. This time the Indian ponies weren't as upset over a stranger's approach. He got to the rope and moved along it, hunting for Black Velvet.

For a hunting party of five braves, they had a powerful lot of horses. Slocum reckoned they had been doing a little horse stealing along with their deer hunting. One horse carried a brand. Slocum didn't recognize it, but Indians never branded their mustangs. This had come from some Wyoming ranch. It might have been purchased legally, but Slocum doubted it. Big Stump had to realize something was wrong when Quinn sold Black Velvet for a single buffalo hide.

"Buyer beware," Slocum said, a grin slipping from ear to ear when he saw the big black horse. He made his way to it, and fumbled at the knot on Black Velvet's halter to release it. Another horse pawed the ground and snorted angrily. This caused Black Velvet to jerk and try to get away from Slocum.

"Everything's okay, old boy," Slocum said, trying to calm the horse. Black Velvet had been out of the barn only a day and already it had forgotten Slocum. Or had it?

This idea penetrated too slowly to save Slocum. He glanced over his shoulder, caught a glimpse of a rifle barrel swinging through the air, then staggered under the impact. He saw stars, and then keeping his feet under him proved too hard.

But Slocum fought. If he didn't get away now, he would be a dead man.

He dug in his toes and launched forward, not sure who he was hitting. His shoulder crushed into a man's belly, and Slocum thought he had hit a brick wall. He bounced to one side, crashed to the ground, and rolled. The rifle barrel glanced off the top of his head again. This time he was too stunned to get back to his feet. Slocum felt strong hands pulling at him. In the distance Black Velvet neighed in anguish at what was happening.

Slocum wished he had that much strength. He blacked out.

Heat on his face brought him around. Slocum jerked his face away from the firebrand thrust at his eyes. Squinting, he saw the Arapaho hunters were passing a bottle around. He cursed under his breath. Quinn had probably sold them some whiskey when he had given away Black Velvet.

"You're a horse thief," Big Stump said. The Indian stared down at Slocum. The raw end of his left arm gleamed pink and scarred in the dancing firelight.

"That stallion was stolen from a woman in Scorpion Bend."

"Squaws don't own horses. Horses are for warriors!"

Slocum was in no position to argue the point. On the frontier, property ownership laws were more lax than in the cities. Miss Maggie shouldn't own a horse—but no one in town was likely to argue the point. Nor would they argue over her owning a saloon, though it was doubtful the law would let Rachel Decker keep her farm after her pa died.

Land was important. So were horses.

"It was stolen by a man named Quinn," Slocum said. "I came to take it back."

He tugged at the ropes around his wrists. He felt the rough hemp cut into his wrists. Big Stump—or one of the warriors with him—had tied Slocum up too tightly to get free. Trickles of blood ran down his wrists and into the palms of his hands as he tried to rub the rope against the tree trunk.

Slocum was sitting. He pushed, trying to get his feet under him so he could rise with his hands still fastened behind him and around the slender tree trunk. Looking up at Big Stump put him at a disadvantage and made him feel inconsequential.

The Arapaho shoved him down when he tried to stand.

"You tried to steal *my* horse," Big Stump said. The big Indian shoved out his chest and looked truculent.

"What are you going to do?" asked Slocum, but he spoke to empty air. Big Stump had moved away, giving a whoop and beginning to dance around the fire. Within seconds, someone had given him a full quart of whiskey. Within minutes, Big Stump had drained half the quart bottle. He staggered and danced and turned more belligerent as the rotgut took hold of his senses.

Slocum worked furiously to get the ropes free, but his hands went numb on him. Blood ran sluggishly down his wrists now, and he felt his heart hammering hard in his chest. He was getting more scared by the minute, although he knew that unbridled fear would get him killed quick as a wink.

The Arapaho pulled their knives and danced past him, blades swinging as they passed by. The object of their game seemed to be to see how close they could get to him without actually cutting him. Too many times they lost, the keen tips of their knives leaving bloody scratches on his chest and face and arms. Slocum wished he could get one of those knives in his hand, if only for a few seconds.

He realized his hands might not be strong enough to grip the knife, but a blade was his only hope of escape. Or was it? The Arapaho finished a bottle and went back for another one. They had started with a full case. Slocum saw two empty bottles. Five men had split two quarts of tarantula juice. They would either pass out soon, or get so plumb mean they would kill him outright.

Getting the ropes off his hands wasn't possible, but another way of escape might work. Slocum fought to get his feet under him again. This time Big Stump wasn't there to shove him back down. Slocum started walking forward. This put incredible strain on his shoulders as he bent the tree. Limbs cut into his flesh. He ignored the pain. Inch by inch he bent the supple young sapling forward. As he got closer to the top of the tree, his hope soared. Once free, he might get away in the dark. Given a few free minutes, he could get the ropes off.

Then he would play it by ear.

Gritting his teeth, he pulled, ignoring the pressure put on his shoulders as he bent forward and lifted his arms. An instant before success was his, he felt himself being lifted upward. He yelped as he sailed through the air. Big Stump had wrapped arms around him, hefted him, and thrown him upward. That allowed the tree to snap erect again. Slocum ratcheted down the tree, the rough bark cutting into his back and arms. He crashed to the ground hard enough to knock the air out of him.

Big Stump laughed, then stepped aside.

Slocum went cold inside. Two of the hunters stood with arrows nocked on their bows. They loosed their arrows. Slocum felt the world dip into molasses and move at half speed all around him. He clearly saw the metal arrowhead on the left arrow. It came directly for his head, then seemed to veer to one side and vanish into the night.

The other arrow grazed his forehead, leaving yet another bloody scratch to give him pain and rob him of a bit more strength.

Slocum was bleeding to death from half a hundred small cuts. Not one was big enough to disable him, but he felt his feet and arms turning cold as his circulation failed to distribute what blood remained in him.

Big Stump laughed at his misery, and then returned to the fire, dancing, chanting, drinking. Slocum stared at the Arapaho and wondered how much longer he had to live. Big Stump might have only one hand, but he held all the cards.

Slocum sagged, trying to gather enough strength to keep fighting. He had failed to steal Black Velvet back, and now he was going to pay the price for his inept horse thieving.

He lifted his head when he heard a new sound in the night. An owl hooted in the distance and wings flapped, but this was something else. A slithery sound, possibly a snake coming up. He frowned. Was dying from the bite of a timber rattler any worse than letting Big Stump kill him for horse theft?

He tried to get his hands into position to abrade the rope against the tree bark again, but as he moved he heard a low hiss.

"Don't," came the whispered command. "Stay still. Play dead even."

Slocum froze. Cold metal pressed into his damaged wrists. Then the familiar *snick* of a knife parting rope came to his ears. He slumped forward, his hands free. Hastily putting his hands back behind him to keep the Arapaho from seeing he was free, he felt his unseen ally worrying at the bonds still around his wrists.

"How are we going to get out of here?" he asked.

"You need to get a horse. Where's the sorrel?"

Someone knew a powerful lot about him.

"Don't know," Slocum said. He watched the Arapaho

dance. They had slowed and were stumbling around right now. If he made a break, it had to be now. Big Stump would either remember it was time to kill his horse thief or pass out. Either way, Slocum couldn't wait any longer.

He spun around and faced his rescuer. His eyes went wide.

"Rachel!"

"Hush, John. How are we going to get away? I have a horse, but it can't carry us both."

"I lost track where my horse is," Slocum said, looking back over his shoulder. "But I know where Black Velvet is."

"I'll meet you at the Stone Needle," Rachel said.

"Wait," he said, reaching out. His fingers felt like bloated sausages. "I don't know where that is."

"I'll get my horse, and we can both go get Black Velvet," she said.

He grabbed her arm. "Wait," he repeated.

"What now?"

"Thanks," he said, bending over and kissing her. A smile crossed her lips. Then she sobered.

"Hurry, John. I don't think they will notice you're gone, but if they do..."

She didn't have to finish. He wasn't armed, and she couldn't hold off five braves, even if they were drunk as lords.

Slocum and Rachel crept into the night. She tugged on the reins of her horse, then pressed her hand over its nose to keep it quiet.

"Circle wide, then come in on the horses from upslope," Slocum said. "I'll meet you there."

"Where are you going?"

Slocum patted his empty holster. They wouldn't stand much of a chance against the Arapaho if they were discovered. He might run and get away, but he felt better with his trusty Colt Navy weighing down his left hip. Rachel started to protest, then fell silent. She came to a decision and nodded twice, sending a tiny strand of brown hair down into her eyes. She hastily pushed it back into place, then melted into the night.

Slocum zigzagged back through the dark, careful to make no sound. The Arapaho were chanting loudly now and had stopped dancing, possibly because they couldn't stand any longer. Three quarts of whiskey downed this fast ought to have caused the men to pass out. That they still laughed and joked and chanted as they danced told him they were made of stern stuff.

Flat on his belly, Slocum wiggled closer to the fire. To his left hung the venison from the deer the hunters had bagged. To his right were stacked rifles—and his Colt Navy. He grabbed his six-shooter and shoved it into his holster, then took a handful of dirt and funneled as much into each rifle barrel as he could.

It never hurt to buy a little insurance. The dirt might not cause a rifle to blow up if it were fired, but it would certainly cause a bullet to go off target. If Slocum's head was their target, any break he could get would be helpful.

He slithered like a snake back into the night, got to his feet, and made his way as fast as he dared around the camp, coming downhill toward the rope corral where the Arapaho horses stood quietly now. This time the horses accepted him as belonging among them and made no fuss.

"Hello, Black Velvet," he said, stroking the powerful stallion's head. "We're going for a ride, even if I have to ride you bareback."

He spun at a small sound, six-shooter out and ready to fire. Slocum relaxed when he saw Rachel.

"You move like an Indian," he said. "I didn't hear you until you were on top of me."

"That's a pity. Maybe we can do something about that—later," Rachel said. "We head out, go west, and if you see a tall, thin spire of rock, that's Stone Needle.

There's a trail at its base leading across the mountain and into Scorpion Bend."

Slocum wanted to ask her about a shortcut, if Quinn might gain an advantage coming across the mountain rather than sticking with the main race course, but that could come later. He pulled the stallion away, then stopped.

"Your knife," he said. "Let me borrow it."

Rachel tossed it to him. He fielded it easily and lashed out with the blade, slicing through the rope holding the other horses.

"John!"

Slocum already saw the trouble coming at him. Big Stump stumbled along, hefted his rifle, and pointed it at Slocum's head.

With a powerful jump, Slocum got astride Black Velvet and put his heels into the animal's flanks. The powerful black stallion blasted off like a rocket.

Behind him, Slocum heard the hammer fall on the Arapaho's rifle. A muffled *thunk* followed. The dirt poured into the barrel had robbed Big Stump of a good shot.

Now it was up to Slocum and Rachel to get away before the Indian came after them. Drunk or sober, the Arapaho was a formidable opponent—and an angry one, now that Slocum had stolen his prized horse.

15

"I can't go on any longer," Slocum said. He thought of himself as indestructible, and showing any weakness in front of Rachel Decker bothered him more than it ought to. But he could not ride on any longer. The dozens of shallow cuts administered by the Arapaho had mostly clotted over, but he had lost enough blood to weaken him. If this was the only thing, he might have gone on. He had been wounded worse than this and ridden fifty miles the next day. But it was only part of his problem. Slocum couldn't remember when last he had eaten.

On top of all that were the more serious injuries he had accumulated since coming to Scorpion Bend.

The bullet crease he had picked up during the first race—was it really from Frank Decker's bullet or had Quinn lied?—burned across his shoulders like a lightning bolt now. He should have had Doc Marsten properly look after it when he'd had the luxury of a few spare minutes. There had not been the time, and all the booze he had sucked up at Miss Maggie's saloon had killed the pain.

Until now.

He winced as other minor aches and pains poked into him, and he wobbled in the saddle.

"You're hurt," Rachel said. "I didn't know, John. I shouldn't have pushed you this hard."

"I haven't thanked you for saving my hide back there," he said. Slocum blinked and stared ahead. The quarter moon provided only a sliver of light, but against it he saw a knife blade of stone gutting the sky. That had to be the Stone Needle Rachel had said marked the pass through to Scorpion Bend. They were so close to getting across the mountains that he wanted to ride on.

Time, or the lack of it, worried him too. He wasn't sure what time it was, but it might be as late as midnight. How long Big Stump and the other Arapahos had tortured him wasn't something he could judge. It had seemed to last years, but might have been only an hour or so. His judgment was impaired, but he knew at eight o'clock on Saturday morning he had better be on the starting line with Black Velvet under him or there would be hell to pay.

He might not win, but just showing up for the race would be a minor victory over Cletus Quinn. Even that small act of defiance seemed worth any amount of suffering right now.

"We can camp for a few hours in a place I know," Rachel said, glancing over in his direction. She was obviously worried about his condition, but Slocum thought he might look worse than he felt. At least he hoped that was so. Otherwise, all that was left for him was a coffin. "The Stone Needle is only a couple miles off and—"

Rachel cocked her head to one side and gasped.

Slocum heard the same sound she did, and it chilled him. The Arapaho weren't drunk enough or forgiving enough to let him steal Big Stump's new stallion. Hoofbeats sounded not that far behind them—and they were getting closer.

"I can't ride much longer," Slocum said. "We need to find somewhere to make a stand." He felt a surge of energy galvanize him into action. He recognized that it wouldn't last too long and that he had to use it fast. When the vitality faded, he and Rachel had to be safe or they would be dead.

"With what, John? I've got a rifle and half a box of cartridges. Your six-shooter might be fully loaded, but that's all the ammo we have between us."

Less than thirty rounds. In the dark against Indians capable of walking up to an Army sentry without being seen. With him so giddy from blood loss and hunger he could hardly stay upright in the saddle.

It didn't look good for him to please Miss Maggie by showing up for the big race.

"I don't know if I can outrun them," Slocum said. "Black Velvet's willing. I'm not sure I can hang on." Slocum felt Rachel's strong hand supporting him as he sagged. He rode for a hundred yards or more and hardly realized he had done so.

"Get off," Rachel urged. "I'll decoy them, circle, and come back to pick you up."

"I can't let you do that," he said.

"You're in no condition to do much else," Rachel said testily. "I can ride. I can ride better than you."

Slocum noted she didn't add "right now." He was missing something about her, and couldn't concentrate on what it was. But something else came to him that might work.

"You can decoy them, all right," he said. "But we need to do it a little different than you meant. Give me your rifle and the box of ammo."

"What?"

"Do it. Then ride around, get them all hot on your trail, and lead them back by this spot. I'll be ready in a few minutes and waiting for them."

"You're a good enough shot to get an Arapaho hunting party in the dark?" She sounded skeptical.

"I am," he said, and Rachel believed him. Silently, she drew out her rifle from its saddle sheath and handed it to him. It took a few seconds of fumbling in her saddlebags to find the box of cartridges. Slocum bounced it a couple times, listening to the way it rattled. There might not even be half a box.

However many shells there were would have to do or both he and Rachel would end up dead.

He dismounted and led Black Velvet into the rocks. Rachel waited until she made sure she knew where he holed up. She waved, her horse reared, and Slocum watched as she expertly brought the animal back under control. Again he felt he was missing something.

Then Rachel vanished into the night, the thudding of her horse's hooves evident to even a deaf man. Slocum settled down, spread what little he had in the way of weapons and ammunition around him, then shifted position for the best possible attack. It took only a few minutes for Big Stump and his Arapaho brothers to come by. Slocum let them go. They were galloping hard, eager to catch up with Rachel.

When they came back, *then* he would attack. He loaded the rifle's magazine and laid the weapon aside. Then he checked his Colt Navy. He slid it back into his holster so he would always know where it was. He placed the twelve spare cartridges for the rifle near his right hand, then hefted the rifle, got comfortable, and waited.

During the war he had often waited for hours for a single shot. Now he knew he might fall asleep or even pass out if it came to that long an interval. Luckily for him, Rachel came back within twenty minutes, her horse lathered from the run. She looked around, spotted him, and waved, then hurried on, getting into the rocks a dozen yards further down the trail.

Slocum knew what to expect, and reacted more from instinct than awareness of the situation. He let one Arapaho ride past and then another. He shot the third one. As the Indian's horse reared and threw its rider into the two trailing ones, he had time to pick his next target. He was rewarded with a loud shriek of pain when he drilled the second Arapaho. He levered in another round and fired. This round missed, as did the rest in the magazine.

Slocum hastily reloaded while the Indians were wondering where the barrage came from. It took Big Stump only a few more seconds to pinpoint Slocum's location and charge. Slocum emptied his rifle fast, using the last of Rachel's ammo. He whipped out his six-shooter and fired almost point-blank into Big Stump's face. He missed again, but the powder set fire to the Indian's hair, forcing him back.

Big Stump rode into the night, hair on fire. Slocum turned to the others and fired with as much precision as he could until his Colt's hammer landed on a spent chamber. He was out of ammunition.

He waited to deal with the Arapaho in hand-to-hand fighting, but the space in front of him was empty. The scent of burned powder filled the crisp night air. The Arapaho were gone.

Slocum sank to the ground, shaking uncontrollably. By the time Rachel rode up, he had recovered enough to slide down the rock and stand beside her.

"That was fantastic, John," she said. "You ran them all off. I'd've bet against you doing it with only a few rounds, but—"

"I doubt they will be back. I hope Big Stump thinks he tangled with a powerful spirit."

"Big Stump?"

"The Arapaho leader."

"You surely did find out a lot about them. I ought to follow you around to see what else you know."

She dismounted and came toward him. Slocum's weakness passed entirely now that she was close. She came into his arms. For a moment they stared into each other's eyes. Then they kissed. The world closed in around Slocum and became filled only with the sweetness of her lips, the warmth of her body pressing into his, and other urges growing in his loins.

"I'll get my bedroll," she said, breaking off the kiss.

"We ought to get back to Scorpion Bend. I have to be there before the race starts."

"So do I," she said. "And we'll have plenty of time. I've ridden the trail often enough to know. Once we get to the Stone Needle, it is only an hour to the middle of town." She went to her horse and fumbled at the leather thongs holding her bedroll over the horse's hindquarters. Again Slocum groped for the detail that was eluding him, that was making him feel as if his brain was itching, and then he was occupied with something far more intimate and enjoyable.

The ground under the blanket wasn't soft, but enough loose dirt provided Slocum padding so he could stretch out flat on his back without too much discomfort. Rachel floated above him like an angel, the dim moonlight catching and highlighting her brown hair with silver. She worked to peel his shirt off. The dried blood had caused the fabric to stick to his flesh. Rachel's eyes went wider when she saw all the tiny, dark grooves in his hide.

"No," he said, reaching up and pressing his fingers against her lips. He didn't want to hear what she thought of his bloodied body. His finger moved along the line of her jaw, and then slid down the front of her blouse. One by one the fancy bone buttons came free. Her breasts tumbled out to bob about slightly, delightful mounds of quicksilver in the night. Gripping them, stroking, squeezing, Slocum roved over them until Rachel moaned with pleasure.

She bent over and their lips met again. Then Rachel arched her back and presented her breasts to him for oral attention. Slocum licked and kissed and suckled until the woman's body trembled like a frisky filly.

He shucked off her blouse entirely and dropped it beside them. She took a few seconds to get free of the rest of her clothing while he wiggled free of his jeans.

"Is this the Stone Needle?" she asked, reaching down to his groin. "It's hard enough. But it's so warm."

"No, no, it's not made out of rock," Slocum said. "And it's cold. I want it to be where it's warm and damp."

"Here?" Rachel stepped over him and settled down over his waist again. Her naked crotch brushed against his erection until she reached down and took him in hand. Rachel guided the thick stalk to her nether lips and positioned it. She wiggled back and forth and fitted him perfectly into her most intimate recess. Slocum sighed in pleasure as he was surrounded by clutching female flesh.

Rachel arched her back and began undulating, moving above him, letting his manhood slide back and forth within her. Slocum reached up to her breasts and squeezed down hard. He caught the rock-hard nubs and pressed down on them. This drove Rachel wild with need.

"Yes, John, yes. It fills me with such desire! I need it all. I do, I do!"

She gasped and moaned and began moving faster and faster. Slocum felt warmth mounting in his loins, spreading and threatening to explode at any instant. She sobbed, and pressed down on his chest with her hands to get better leverage.

Her hips slammed down hard into him, and they both approached the point of no return. When Rachel erupted, so did Slocum. The woman sank down and laid her cheek against his, their bodies still pressed together intimately. Then Rachel shivered.

"It's going to be a cold night," she said.

"Not if we're together," Slocum said. He moved over and made room for the woman in the folds of the blanket. The ground was still hard, but he didn't think he would mind. Rachel was warm and soft against him. Between lovemaking and all the rest that had happened to him, Slocum fell asleep quickly and deeply.

He awoke with a start a few hours later. Rachel murmured at the way he jerked about, but remained asleep, her hot, regular breath gusting gently against his bare shoulder. Slocum rolled so he could hold her and study the stars above them.

He found the summer stars he used to tell time. He reckoned that it was three or four in the morning. The race in Scorpion Bend was only about four hours off, but he felt better for the short nap—and Rachel. He was hungry and his body hurt as if he had fallen into an anthill and been repeatedly bitten, but he felt better, especially with Rachel beside him under the blanket.

His belly growled in hunger, forcing him to get up. He made sure Rachel was under the blanket as he went to her horse. If she had brought along a box of cartridges and a bedroll, she might also have some jerky or something else he could eat. It bothered him a little that they had not taken off the saddle to give the horse a rest, but Slocum wasn't going to wrestle with it right now. Not until he found what he was hunting for in Rachel's saddlebags.

He soothed the skittish horse as he rummaged through the left saddlebag. All that was in it was some dusty clothing. He looked through the other bag, finally finding a strip of jerky so old it was growing mold. To him it looked better than a fine Delmonico steak. Slocum's mouth puckered when he bit into the salty, moldy meat. He looked for Rachel's canteen.

The horse reared and shook all over, causing some of the clothing from the saddlebags to fall to the ground.

"There, there," Slocum said, soothing the horse. He went back around and picked up a floppy, big-brimmed hat. And a bandanna. And a tan duster.

Slocum stepped back a pace and stared at the horse, studying it carefully for the first time. He finally realized what had been eating away at him and what he had not realized until this moment. Slocum tried to pass it off as being wounded and hungry and bone-tired. Then he knew the truth was a lot simpler. He had simply denied what he probably had known for a long time.

The horse shied away from him again.

He laid his hand on its head and gentled it. "There, there, Pilot," he said. "Don't worry. You'll make it to Scorpion Bend in time for the race."

16

Slocum spun around when he heard movement behind him. Rachel, the blanket pulled snugly around her shoulders, eyed him and the telltale clothing that had tumbled from her saddlebags. The expression on her lovely face was unreadable. Then she smiled almost shyly.

"I wondered when you would figure it out."

Slocum knew he should not have been going through her saddlebags. He held out the uneaten portion of the beef jerky. Rachel shook her head, then sat on a rock and simply stared at him.

"I've been busy with other things," he said. "I owe you a thank-you many times over."

"You should never have ridden into that rope trap. That was a real greenhorn stunt," she said, smiling. "I'm not sure why I bothered freeing you. I'm glad I did."

"I am too," Slocum said. He sat beside her, their bodies pressing together for warmth. A quick swig of water from the canteen assuaged his thirst. Rachel took it and drank more deeply. He finished the jerky. It was hardly enough to keep his belly from complaining that his throat was cut.

"What are you going to do?" she asked.

"I don't understand," Slocum said. "What am I going to do about what?"

"About me being Pilot. I guess it was foolish for me to go by my horse's name. When I paid my registration money, they asked for a name, and that was all I could think of. I was pretty scared then."

"Where'd you get the hundred dollars?"

Rachel shrugged. The blanket fell off one white shoulder. He pulled it back up and moved even closer to her. Warmth from her seeped into his body and renewed him.

"I barely had enough money to eat on, much less use to register for the race," she said. "And then Frank stole what little I had left for his drinking and gambling spree." She gave a harsh laugh. "If he hadn't squandered it, I would have bet the whole wad on me. That would have been a waste, I know, but—"

"Why a waste?" he interrupted. "You stand a good chance to win. Pilot's a strong horse, and you're a good rider."

"Going against Quinn and his henchmen was a risk, but I reckoned I could beat them with a little luck," she said. "But against you? I've seen you ride. You're the best, and Black Velvet is the perfect horse for you. That's an unbeatable combination."

Slocum didn't feel unbeatable at the moment. He didn't ache as much as he had, but he still felt weak as a kitten. And hungry! He could eat a whole cow, moo and all.

"We'll get to town in time to start," Slocum promised. "I admire the way you're doing this for your pa."

"I don't have any choice. If I don't get the money to pay the mortgage, I lose the farm. Pa's days are numbered, and I've about run out of people to ask to come in to stay with him while I'm out working—or racing."

Slocum understood that. No one in the countryside would want to watch after an invalid during the biggest race of the year. Such excitement would draw the people like flies to honey.

"I'm leaving him by himself. He doesn't get up, so if he's got some food and water before I leave, he ought to be fine. But I don't feel good about it."

"We all do what we have to," Slocum said.

Rachel stared at him, her brown eyes wide and shining in the light of the setting moon. "You'll beat me if you have the chance, won't you?"

He nodded. To his surprise, she kissed him hard.

"I wouldn't want it any other way." She kissed him again. Then Rachel pulled back and said, "But you're going to have to ride like the wind to beat me, John Slocum!"

"Maybe I should try getting you all tuckered out first." He kissed her. They sank to the ground. Rather than wearing one another out, they fed each other's energy and determination.

Slocum dropped to the ground outside the stable. Two men stared at him, not sure what to say or do. One finally turned and ran off. Slocum knew he was going to tell Miss Maggie both horse and rider were back.

"Get me some food," Slocum ordered the other man. "And get someone to tend the horse. I need the saddle and other gear ready for the race."

"That's in an hour, Mr. Slocum."

"Then you better get to jumping," Slocum said sharply. He and Rachel had ridden into town. Every yard closer to Scorpion Bend he had become edgier and edgier, until he was ready to snap at everyone. He knew what the race meant to Rachel—and to Miss Maggie, and to the dozens of others betting on it. Letting Quinn win with no opposition wasn't his way of doing things, but Slocum was realistic about his chances.

He had been battered, beaten, and starved. Black Velvet needed a rest. And Quinn would stop at nothing to win. Any trick, no matter how low-down, was possible.

The one good thing Slocum had gained by returning to Scorpion Bend with Rachel was finding out the passes across the mountain and back to the valley where the Arapaho had been hunting. Taking the Stone Needle trail cut miles and miles off the race. As long as he checked in with judges scattered sporadically along the way, and started and finished at the same line in town, no one cared what route he rode.

Slocum knew he would be fighting Cletus Quinn every inch of this trail.

"Slocum, you decided to show up. I thought you had gunned down Jed and hidden his body after stealing Black Velvet." The saloon owner stood in the door of the stable, hands on her flaring hips. She had blood in her eye, and acid dripped from her words.

"It was Quinn's doing," Slocum said. He was in no mood to explain to Miss Maggie all he had been through. "It's going to be a real surprise for him when he sees me show up for the race—on Black Velvet." Slocum patted the stallion. Black Velvet nickered softly, then returned to the bag of oats the stable hand had given the horse.

"So I should bet my life on this?"

"Why not? You already bet the saloon," he said. This got a laugh from Miss Maggie.

"Jed hightailed it because he thought you wouldn't get the horse back from Quinn?" She shook her head sadly. "I thought better of him. Unless he helped Quinn steal the horse."

"I don't think he had anything to do with it. The horse theft was Quinn's idea. He sold it to an Arapaho named Big Stump for a single buffalo blanket."

"Son of a bitch," Miss Maggie said. Her lips thinned to a determined line. "I'll see you get some victuals."

"And have Doc Marsten stop by. I'm in need of some patching," Slocum said.

Miss Maggie eyed his shirt, sniffed in disdain, and said, "Those puny little cuts? You're turning into a cream puff, Slocum." She left the stable, but the doctor bustled in less than ten minutes later, obviously summoned by the saloon keeper.

Slocum ate a good breakfast, winced as the doctor worked on his cuts and sores, then tried to convince himself he would beat Quinn in the race. He knew he wasn't up against only Quinn. Zachary and Bloomington were his cronies, and would willingly sacrifice their chances at winning so their boss could win. Slocum wondered if anyone had bet on either of those men. If so, the bettor was probably drunk or didn't have eyes to see how it was.

Quinn and his cohorts made up three of the five riders in the final. That made Quinn the odds-on favorite.

Slocum saddled Black Velvet, made sure he gave the horse a couple lumps of sugar he had not put into his black coffee, then mounted. Doc Marsten looked up at him.

"You get on out there and win, Slocum. I don't want all my work going for naught." The doctor wiped his hands on his pants legs, closed his case, and hurried off to get a good view of the start.

"I'll win," Slocum said softly, more to himself than to the doctor. He put his heels to Black Velvet's flanks, and the powerful horse jumped forth, ready to race. Slocum cantered to the street and paused there, staring at the start line.

The canvas banner over the street flapped fitfully in the wind. A huge crowd had already gathered around Cletus Quinn. The man sat astride his horse, facing away from Slocum, boasting about how he was going to win.

"Bet heavy, gents," Quinn cried. "Bet against me if you want to lose, bet on me if you want to get rich!"

Zachary and Bloomington were astride their horses a few yards off. No one paid them any mind. And at the far end of the dusty street Slocum saw that Rachel was ready to make another of her running starts. She tugged at her red bandanna and settled her duster. He had no problem now recognizing her for the woman she was. How he had missed it before, he still couldn't explain.

But no one expected a woman to enter the Scorpion Bend big race, much less qualify for the final five.

"I'll be back here ten minutes 'fore I start, I'm going to ride so fast," bragged Quinn.

"Then you'll be too slow by half and eating my dust all the way," Slocum said in a voice that cut like steel. Deathly silence fell; then the crowd let out a huge cheer. They wanted a race.

Slocum took pleasure in the way Quinn turned pasty white under his weathered tan. The gunman started to say something, but no words came out. He clamped his mouth shut and stared hotly at Slocum. If looks could have killed, Slocum would have been dead in the sun then and there.

It took more than Quinn could dish out to get rid of John Slocum.

"Any time you want to start, let's do it," Slocum said. This brought forth another cheer from the crowd. The starter raised his gun and fired.

Before the finger came back on the trigger and the blast cut through the morning air, Slocum heard Pilot's hooves pounding hard. Rachel Decker blasted past the other four racers and headed out of town amid even louder cheers urging her on.

Slocum stayed neck and neck with Quinn and the other two until he saw they were killing their horses trying to overtake Rachel. He eased back on Black Velvet, letting the stallion fall into a steady run just shy of a full gallop. No horse could gallop endlessly. A mile, definitely. Two miles? Possibly. Three miles? Buzzard bait.

The dust cloud from the others' hooves choked Slocum. He veered off the road and found a grassy stretch better suited to the steady pace he wanted to maintain. Black Velvet responded eagerly, giving Slocum the stride and power he wanted. By cutting off the road, he eliminated a horseshoe bend and found himself slightly ahead of Bloomington, but still lagging both Zachary and Quinn.

"You . . . gonna . . . pay for what . . . you done," Bloomington gasped out.

Slocum figured the man was referring to the gunfight up in the meadow while he was tracking the Arapaho hunting party.

"He was my brother!"

As Bloomington shouted, he swung a length of rope that whistled back for Slocum's face. The attack took him by surprise, and the sharp pain in his cheek where the rope cut him almost knocked him from the saddle. As it was, he leaned to one side, putting Black Velvet off balance. The horse stumbled and recovered.

By then, Bloomington was a dozen yards ahead. The man swung his rope around and around as if it were a whip. Slocum even heard the crack as Bloomington snapped it hard. Getting past the rider would be hard because he would take out Slocum and to hell with any of the judges spotting it.

Bloomington would be disqualified—but so what? He would prevent Slocum from challenging Quinn. Bloomington was nothing more than an expendable pawn in a bigger game.

Bending low, Slocum slowly narrowed the distance between them. At the side of the road he saw dozens of men, all wearing the yellow ribbons of judges tied around their arms. Many waved. Others made obscene gestures. It didn't take much to know which were Miss Maggie's supporters—and his—and which favored Cletus Quinn.

"Comin' back for more, Slocum? Good. I ain't finished punishin' you!" Again Bloomington swung his rope. This time Slocum was expecting it. His hand moving like lighting, he reached out for it. A sharp pain lanced into the tough palm of his left hand and echoed all the way up to his shoulder.

Slocum grabbed tight and hung on. He shoved his heels forward and reared back on Black Velvet. The horse dug in its hooves, kicking up a cloud of dust.

Bloomington's fall from his horse was hidden by the thick cloud. He had been dragged from the saddle, and lay stunned in the center of the road. His eyes had gone unfocused, and he gasped harshly as his lungs tried to recover a measure of the wind knocked from them.

Slocum flicked the rope and looped it around the fallen man's wrist. Then he wrapped the end of the rope he still held around his saddlehorn.

"Giddyup," he commanded Black Velvet. The horse started, balked at the weight it was dragging, then adjusted to be able to pull Bloomington along the road.

Slocum didn't want to exhaust his stallion. He only pulled Bloomington a dozen yards before unfastening the rope from his saddlehorn and tossing it to the ground.

He picked up the pace then, knowing Rachel, Quinn, and Zachary were likely more than a mile ahead of him by now. They had been flying. Slocum worried they might do something to Rachel to take her out of the race, but she would be wary of any tricks. She had even avoided the snares that had almost doomed Slocum in the first race.

The knots of men checking to be sure the race was fair and square flashed by Slocum. He approached the trail over the mountain and hesitated. If he continued, the bend in the road would swing him out and back, adding miles to the racecourse. Or he could head for the Stone Needle and follow the path Rachel had shown him.

He would be alone on the main course. He would face possible ambush following Quinn through the mountain pass and back.

He didn't want anything to happen to Rachel. This

decided him—and the chance to lock horns with Quinn. Slocum had taken his time cleaning and reloading his Colt Navy. Whether to carry a rifle had been a hard decision. He had finally opted for less weight and more speed over the chance he would have to use a long gun against Quinn.

Slocum doubted Quinn would have someone like Frank Decker posted to ambush any of the others this time. He would overestimate the ability of Bloomington and Zachary to provide ample protection to ensure his win. Slocum doubted Quinn knew Bloomington was already out of the race, making the race more even.

Or as even as Slocum was likely to see it with Rachel trying desperately to win. If she failed, she lost her pa's farm. That might just provide her with more gumption to win than Quinn's need to finish first.

It might also prod her into doing something foolish.

Slocum turned off the main road, found the trail across the mountains, and in minutes spotted the sharp tip of the Stone Needle ahead. The pass was steep in places, forcing Slocum to take it slower than he preferred. He presented a good target for anyone in the rocks on either side. But Zachary was nowhere to be seen—and it was from Zachary that Slocum expected his most dangerous opposition.

As he started down the far side of the pass, Slocum spotted dust clouds in the valley beyond. Enough for three horses, but somehow he believed only two raced on. Quinn and Rachel? Or Quinn and Zachary?

He wended his way down sharp switchbacks in the trail, got to the valley floor, and started off, varying Black Velvet's pace to rest the horse but cover the most distance possible.

He had ridden only a mile when he saw Pilot cropping grass. His heart turned to ice.

"Rachel!" he called. "What's happened?"

"John, here. Please, please help me."

She lay in a shallow gully, clutching her leg.

He dismounted and let Black Velvet go to graze alongside Pilot, but the stallion found water and began drinking. Slocum had to tend to Rachel fast or the stallion would bloat himself and the race would be over.

"What kind of trouble have you gotten yourself into this time?" he asked. He got his arm around her and lifted her from the gully. Mud ran down the front of her duster. She tried to walk on her right leg, but it gave way under her.

"Zachary—it was Zachary. I don't know what he used, but there was a bright flash that spooked Pilot. When Pilot reared, I was thrown off. I think I broke my leg."

Slocum worked swiftly, fingers probing. He tried to ignore her sobs of pain. He looked up at her.

"No bones broken, but it is a nasty sprain."

"Then I can ride."

"It'll hurt like hell. Controlling your horse is going to be hard too."

"I'm not going to let that son of a bitch beat me!"

"I'll help you up."

"John?" Rachel stared at him, brown eyes wide. "You don't have to do this. He's going to beat us both if you waste much time with me."

"You first, then him," Slocum said.

Rachel hesitated. "You'd let him win just to help me out?"

"Looks that way," Slocum allowed.

"I thought you were a decent man, but I've been wrong too many times before. Now I know." Rachel smiled almost shyly at him. "There's another shortcut, one Quinn can't know about. My farm juts up on the end of this valley. We go down the stream that runs across my place and it'll put us back on the road into Scorpion Bend."

"How much riding will that save?"

"Five miles," she said. "We can't tarry, but we can still beat him."

"Let's ride," he said, boosting her into the saddle. Rachel settled down and wiggled her feet in the stirrups. She made a face as pain hit her.

"Get some rope and tie my right foot into the stirrup," she said. "It's all swole up and going numb on me. I need to be sure it doesn't slip free when I can least afford it."

"Be better to cut your boot off," Slocum said, but he did as she asked. "It's dangerous riding like that. Get thrown again and your horse can drag you for miles."

"As long as he drags me across the finish line first," Rachel said with fire. She wheeled Pilot around and took off. Slocum pulled Black Velvet from the water and headed after her. They kept up a fast pace most of the morning. By the time the sun beat down smack on the top of his head, they'd recrossed the mountains.

As good as her word, the road they needed to cross the finish line in Scorpion Bend stretched in front of them. It was a considerable run for tired horses and even more tired riders, almost five miles, but nowhere along its dusty length did Slocum see Quinn or Zachary.

"There they come," Rachel said. "We had better try to outrun them."

Black Velvet was strong, but not up to a full gallop. Slocum didn't think Pilot was able to give enough effort for five miles either.

"Pace yourself," Slocum said. He reached over and rested his hand on his six-shooter, just in case. "May the best man win!"

"May the best *woman* win!" cried Rachel. She set a faster pace than Slocum wanted. He held back, conserving Black Velvet's strength for the last mile into town. Slocum thought that was where the race would be won or lost.

And then he found himself dodging and ducking as

rifle bullets sailed past his head. Riding low, looking back, he saw Zachary with a rifle pulled up to his shoulder and squeezing off one round after another. On a running horse, the man had no chance of accurately aiming. But that wasn't necessarily what he wanted to do. Slowing Slocum so Quinn could win drove Zachary's wild attack.

Black Velvet couldn't maintain the even, powerful stride it took to outdistance Zachary, so Slocum slid his six-gun from its holster and let up on the horse. The black stallion slowed and Zachary pulled closer, fumbling with his rifle.

"Did a round jam?" Slocum called. Zachary called something to him that Slocum didn't understand. Slocum's finger pulled back on the trigger of his six-shooter, but he simply could not blow the man out of the saddle.

With a howl of rage, Zachary sawed at his horse's reins and rode across Slocum's path. Black Velvet shied as Zachary swung his rifle like a club.

"Judges are watching," Slocum shouted.

"To hell with them. To hell with you!"

They rode shoulder to shoulder, Slocum trying to avoid the man's wild swings. From behind Slocum heard the pounding of hooves. Cletus Quinn blazed past, laughing as he went. This infuriated Slocum. He lifted his six-shooter, ready to cock and fire it at the gunman's back.

Zachary's rifle barrel crashed to his wrist, numbing his hand. Slocum fought to keep from dropping his six-shooter. He swung away from Zachary, but Quinn's henchman followed like a bad odor. They crisscrossed from one side of the road to the other, Zachary trying to unseat Slocum and Slocum trying to outdistance the man. His chance at shooting Zachary out of the saddle had passed. Slocum's hand was too numb to hope he could hold the six-shooter, much less fire accurately from a running horse at a moving target.

"Gotcha!" Zachary cried in triumph, getting close

enough to Slocum to swing the rifle barrel. Slocum ducked; Zachary missed and lost his balance. He clung fiercely to his saddle. Slocum saw deep grooves in the saddle leather where Zachary's fingernails dug in to keep him mounted.

Slocum helped him. Just a little.

His boot shot out and hooked Zachary's. The man gave a cry of fear and fell under his horse's hooves. The sound of a heavy horse tromping on human flesh might have sickened Slocum had he cared one whit. Zachary was a backshooter and did Quinn's dirty work for him.

He deserved what he got.

And Slocum deserved to win the race.

"Come on, Black Velvet. Give me everything you've got."

Without Zachary hammering at his head, Slocum rode more easily. The hot Wyoming wind rushed past and took off his hat. He never noticed as he squinted into the sun. Quinn had worn out his horse getting over the mountain and taking a longer route than either Rachel or Slocum.

The lack of stamina now told on Quinn's horse. Slocum closed the gap inch by inch.

Less than a mile from the finish line, Slocum heard the cheers going up. He doubted those cries of glee were for any one rider. They were to spur on all the riders, to make this a race everyone in Scorpion Bend would talk about for the next year—and maybe compare all future races to.

"I won't let you take it, Slocum. I won't!" Quinn grated out.

Slocum laughed and slowly passed Quinn. Then Slocum saw Quinn was not the only competition in the race. Ahead, much nearer the finish line, rode Rachel astride Pilot. He saw how she struggled along. By now her sprained ankle had probably swollen to such an extent that pain would be lancing all the way up her leg and into her hips. But however much pain she felt, it didn't keep her from doing her best. She rode Pilot better than any cowboy Slocum had ever known.

"Noooo!" cried Quinn when he saw two were in front of him. He was not going to finish second to Slocum. He would come in third behind Slocum and an anonymous rider. This was the worst ignominy that could happen to him.

Roars of delight went up from the crowd as Slocum and Rachel fought for the win. Slocum wasn't sure who crossed the line first, but he did know they were both long seconds ahead of Quinn. Win or lose to Rachel, he did not care.

He had beaten Quinn honestly.

"You did it, Slocum, you made me a rich woman! You won the race by a nose!" shrieked Miss Maggie. This was the most excited he had ever seen the saloonkeeper. She clapped him on the shoulder and hands reached for him to carry him around Scorpion Bend on the shoulders of the crowd. Slocum pushed them away.

Shouting, he called to Miss Maggie, "Black Velvet. I want the horse taken care of!"

"Done!" she shouted back.

And then Slocum let himself be swallowed up by the crowd. He wondered where Rachel had gone. Slocum wanted to find her for a proper celebration, one that had nothing to do with a hundred drunken cowboys and ranch hands.

17

"Slocum, you did it, you beat that sidewinder!" Miss Maggie crowed. She shoved a bottle of whiskey across the bar toward him. He wondered if she would bother replacing Jed. The barkeep had lit out for the hills when it looked as if Slocum would never recover Black Velvet in time for the race, but he was only another one for Miss Maggie to pay off had he stayed in Scorpion Bend.

"I had some help," Slocum admitted.

"I tried to do what I could giving you the best damn horse in all Wyoming!" Miss Maggie worked the bar, moving from one end to the other, pouring drinks and raking in the money.

Slocum sipped his whiskey. What had once tasted good to him now left a bitter tang. He had won, but if it hadn't been for Rachel Decker he would still be out there riding. Hell, if it hadn't been for the lovely woman, he would never have qualified to be in the second race. He was feeling poorly for having beaten her, even if he felt a warm spot for having ridden the best he could and winning the race.

It wasn't in him to lose, even for a good cause like saving Rachel's farm. He touched his pocket. He vaguely remembered he had cashed in three tickets on himself, probably when he was more than a little drunk. He had three thousand dollars from selling them, and the other two he had given Rachel to cash in. He wouldn't rake in the money from the pot, but he had no complaint.

Still, if he had kept all the tickets he would be twenty-five hundred dollars richer. It hardly seemed to matter if he had won or simply cashed in early. Moreover, he would get what Miss Maggie had promised him to ride Black Velvet to victory. Another thousand dollars on top of the thousand for qualifying for the final race.

"I'm walking away with purty near five thousand dollars," he mused aloud. "I'm richer than I've ever been."

"Slocum, come on back here. I want you to climb up on the table so's I can announce the winner formally," Miss Maggie said.

Slocum was reluctant to climb onto the shaky table for reasons other than the shaky legs. The tent saloon was filled with a hundred or more men. Nowhere did he see Cletus Quinn or any of his henchmen, but that didn't mean they weren't there—and rising above the crowd would make Slocum a perfect target.

Hands grabbed at him and pushed him to the table.

"Gents, here's the new champion of the Scorpion Bend race!" Miss Maggie cried. A cheer went up that deafened Slocum.

"He beat all the others fair and square, and he made a lot of us richer 'n thieves." This caused a ripple of laughter to go through the crowd. "Slocum, here's what you won," Miss Maggie said, handing him a fat envelope. "I already took out my share for lettin' you ride the best damn horse in the entire West."

Another cheer went up, and Miss Maggie declared free drinks to honor Black Velvet. Another round honored Slocum. And another for something Slocum didn't catch. It hardly mattered. Everyone in the saloon intended to get drunk celebrating.

He jumped down and found a chair at the rear of the

tent. He leafed through the winnings. As expected, Miss Maggie had kept all but the promised thousand dollars as her share of letting him ride Black Velvet. That didn't bother him. Buying and selling the tickets on himself had given him a huge lump of money. He still had made money.

Lots of it.

The envelope with his earnings weighed him down something fierce.

"Where you going, John?" Miss Maggie called.

"Be right back," he said. Slocum stepped outside. It was getting near five o'clock. He hurried down the street to the bank. The banker was closing up. The man smiled at Slocum and greeted him by name. This was what fame meant, being recognized by ordinary people, and Slocum wasn't sure he cottoned much to that.

"You have a minute to do some business?" Slocum asked.

"I reckon you've got a pile to put into my bank. For you, Mr. Slocum, I have plenty of time."

Slocum sank down into a chair, his mind racing. "I don't want to put money in. I want to pay off a mortgage."

"You don't have one with this bank. I don't understand."

"The Decker place. How much is owed on it?"

"You want to pay off Decker's debt?" The banker heaved a sigh. "I could be a real jackass and steal a wad of money, but I won't do it, Mr. Slocum. The mortgage got paid in full about an hour back."

"How's that?"

"Miss Decker paid it in full. I suspect she had a big bet on the race and it paid off for her."

"I see," Slocum said, realizing she had cashed in the pair of tickets he had given her. That was fine with him, but he wished he had been able to get the simple pleasure out of doing more for her. He had, after all, beaten her in the race, and that made him feel like he owed her something more than money.

"I can set up a nice account for you. Maybe you'd like to buy some land around the valley? Scorpion Bend is a fine place to settle down. With a grubstake like yours, you could become one of the biggest ranchers in Wyoming."

"I'll hang onto my money for a while longer. Thanks," Slocum said. He left the disgruntled banker to stew in his bad luck at failing to snare all of Slocum's winnings.

In the street, the hot afternoon wind had kicked up, turning Slocum's skin dry and his throat even drier. He considered returning to Miss Maggie's saloon, but too many cowboys crowded in there for his taste. Besides, he wanted to find Rachel.

She had vanished after finishing second to him. He wanted to talk to her and explain, although she seemed to have done all right for herself. Slocum headed for the stable. His sorrel was probably Big Stump's new mount. That irritated him, but he had lost horses before. With the money riding in his shirt pocket, he could buy a decent horse. He considered seeing if Miss Maggie would sell Black Velvet. That was a dependable horse and one he appreciated.

Heading back to talk to Miss Maggie about it, Slocum slowed and then stopped when he saw Cletus Quinn out in the street. The man was squared off and ready to throw down. Slocum slid the keeper off the hammer of his Colt Navy, knowing the showdown was going to happen.

"You cheated me out of my win, Slocum. I shoulda won the race."

"Who's the cheater? Who tried to snare me and have me gunned down by snipers?" asked Slocum.

Quinn laughed harshly. "It still galls you Frank Decker worked for me, don't it?"

"Not as much as it galls me you killed him." Slocum

reached slowly to his pocket and pulled out the silver concho he had found in the hotel room outside the balcony where Frank Decker had been gunned down. "This yours?" Slocum held it up so it caught the late afternoon sunlight. The brilliant silver flash might have dazzled Quinn. If the man had flinched, Slocum would have drawn. The reflection didn't hit the gunman's eyes, so Slocum held his ground.

"Wondered where I'd lost that," said Quinn.

"I found it by Decker's body. After you murdered him."

"So I killed him. He tried to double-cross me. I even caught him betting against me!"

"You lost the race, Quinn. Nothing's going to change that."

"No, but gunning you down will make me feel a damned sight better!"

Slocum glanced past Quinn to the entrance of the tent saloon. A half-dozen men had overheard Quinn's boasts—and confession. Miss Maggie now joined them. The men whispered to her. She vanished back into the saloon.

"This'll be a first for you, won't it, Quinn? Actually trying to shoot an armed man who knows you're coming for him."

"You miserable—" Quinn went for his hogleg. Slocum saw the tension in the man's shoulders, and was already going for his own six-shooter when a shot rang out, staggering Quinn.

Quinn fell to the side, and Slocum's slug ripped through the air where the gunman had been standing.

Miss Maggie stood in the door flap of her saloon, a smoking six-gun in her hand. "Get that varmint, boys. You heard him say he murdered Frank Decker. No need to trouble the marshal or call in the circuit judge, now is there?"

Slocum started to protest. He hated lynch mobs, having

been on the wrong end of their ropes too often for comfort. But he slid his six-shooter back into its holster and let the half-drunk crowd carry the wounded Cletus Quinn away, intent on stringing him up as part of Scorpion Bend's festivities.

"He was a bad apple, Slocum," Miss Maggie told him. "I overheard him say he'd killed Frank Decker. Decker was a wastrel, but he didn't deserve to be murdered, not by the likes of Cletus Quinn."

"Reckon Quinn's boys will be moving on real quiet-like," Slocum said. He saw a pair of men he recognized as having ridden with Quinn arguing between themselves. Then they mounted and rode off—in the opposite direction of the lynch mob.

"It's always more peaceful after the race," Miss Maggie said. "You stayin' or you goin'?"

Slocum dickered with her for Black Velvet, and ended up paying her five hundred dollars for the sturdy stallion.

"I'm gonna miss your ugly face around here, Slocum," Miss Maggie said. "There'll be someone else who misses you too."

Slocum stared in the direction of the Decker farm. He had not realized Miss Maggie had known about his involvement with Rachel.

"She rode real good in the race too. If you hadn't been astride Black Velvet, she'd've won."

"You know about everything, don't you?"

"It comes with the territory," Miss Maggie said, grinning broadly. " 'Fore you ride on, wherever fortune takes you, stop by and tell her good-bye."

Slocum touched the brim of his new Stetson and rode off. He heard the loud neigh of a horse and a dull snapping sound. Quinn wouldn't ruffle anyone's feathers in Scorpion Bend again.

It took longer to reach the farm than he thought, possibly because he rode so slowly. Slocum had no idea what he wanted to say to Rachel, but knew he had to say something.

"Wondered if you'd be by, John. Thought you might," said Rachel's soft voice. He turned and saw her sitting under a thick-boled tree by the road, enjoying the sunset as she waited for him to ride past. He wondered if she had been sitting there long. Probably since the race.

"Mind if I join you?" he asked. "For a while?"

Rachel patted the ground next to her. She watched him as he dismounted and tied Black Velvet to a fence post.

"You bought Black Velvet?" she asked.

"Seemed the thing to do after I lost my sorrel," he said, sitting beside Rachel. The sunset was spectacular. And he knew what he had to say.

"I'm heading up to Bozeman," he said. "There's not much more around here for me."

"No, I suppose not," she said. Silence fell between them, interrupted only by songbirds and the soft whisper of the warm breeze twisting this way and that down the road.

"I paid off the mortgage," Rachel said eventually.

"I know."

Rachel's eyebrows rose. Then she nodded, as if reading his mind about what he had tried to do for her.

"I suspected something of the sort," she said finally. "Thank you, John, but the money came from an honest source. Kind of honest, at least. Miss Maggie paid me almost four thousand dollars off a bet Frank had laid on the race."

"What?"

"Seems he was drunk, which figures, and he bet on the wrong rider. He put everything on you. Miss Maggie figured I, being the only one left in the Decker clan able to use the money, deserved it." Rachel took out a bulging envelope and handed it to him.

"What's this?"

"The money from the two tickets you gave me—to hold for you until after the race."

"You have enough?" He took the envelope. Their fingers touched. Then Rachel drew back. She bit her lower lip and nodded, as if her thoughts were a hundred miles away.

Slocum wondered if Decker had been killed by Quinn because of the bet—or if there had ever been a wager. Knowing Miss Maggie, there might not have been one. She was a good person, deep down.

"Glad things are working out for you," Slocum said.

Rachel heaved a deep sigh. "My pa's no better. No worse either. I can't leave him and I'm not going to move him." Another long silence followed. Rachel continued. "I can't expect you to stay either. As much as I want you to."

Slocum thought of a thousand reasons to stay, but none of them matched the need to keep riding, to find the distant horizon and to see what lay beyond it. He couldn't ask Rachel to abandon her duty to her pa—and he wasn't up to helping her.

"I ought to stay," Slocum said.

"Yes, you ought to," Rachel said, staring at him, her brown eyes wide. "But you can't. I know it, and you know it." She bent over and kissed him lightly. "Come back soon. Things might be different then."

He kissed her back, then mounted Black Velvet and rode off. It was hard not to look back. Slocum knew he could never ride on if he did.

The road was a little lonelier than it might have been, but it was his road.